Bride of the Living Dummy

D1513869

Look for more books in the Goosebumps Series 2000
by R.L. Stine:

Bride of the Living Dummy

R.L. Stine

Hippo

Scholastic Children's Books,
Commonwealth House, 1–19 New Oxford Street, London WC1A 1NU, UK
a division of Scholastic Ltd
London ~ New York ~ Toronto ~ Sydney ~ Auckland
Mexico City ~ New Delhi ~ Hong Kong

First published in the USA by Scholastic Inc., 1998
First published in the UK by Scholastic Ltd, 1998

ISBN 0 590 66089 6

Typeset by Rowland Phototypesetting Ltd, Bury St Edmunds, Suffolk
Printed and bound by Mackays of Chatham

10 9 8 7 6 5

"Jillian — what are you *doing*?"

I heard my sister's squeaky voice from my bedroom doorway. I dropped another dead fly into the glass cage. Petey's pointed pink tongue shot out and lapped it up.

"Mmmmm. Juicy fly meat," I murmured to him. "Nice and rare."

"What are you doing?" Katie repeated.

I turned to the door. "I'm practising the violin," I told her.

Katie made a disgusted face. "No, you're not. You're feeding that lizard."

"Duh," I replied, rolling my eyes. I held up a dead fly. "Want a snack? Yum, yum."

"That lizard is gross," she moaned.

"I like him," I insisted. I reached into the cage and tickled Petey under his flat, leathery chin. "It's late. Why are you still up?" I asked my sister.

She yawned. "I'm not tired," she replied.

1

Amanda, Katie's twin, stepped into the room. "I'm not tired, either," she declared. "And neither is Mary-Ellen. Mary-Ellen wants us to stay up till midnight!"

I groaned. "Get Mary-Ellen out of my room, please," I said through gritted teeth.

"Mary-Ellen can go wherever she wants!" Amanda insisted.

"Mary-Ellen doesn't like you, Jillian," Katie added with a sneer. "She hates you and she hates your lizard!"

"Well, I hate Mary-Ellen!" I cried. "Get her out of my room!"

I know, I know. I was being as babyish as my six-year-old sisters. But I can't help it. I really do hate Mary-Ellen.

Ever since Dad brought Mary-Ellen home, life here at the Zinman house has been difficult.

Mary-Ellen is a huge doll, almost as tall as the twins. She has frizzy brown hair made out of mop yarn. A red, heart-shaped mouth twisted up in a sick grin. Strange violet-coloured glass eyes. And ugly blood-red circles painted on her round cheeks.

The doll is a *horror* — but the girls treat her as a third sister. They dress up the doll in their clothes. They talk to her. They sing to her. They pretend to feed her. And they drag her everywhere they go.

They are much nicer to Mary-Ellen than they

2

are to me. At night, I plan horrible things I'm going to do to that disgusting doll.

Amanda slung the big doll over her shoulder. "Mary-Ellen says we can stay up till midnight," she told me.

I slipped another juicy fly into Petey's open mouth. "I don't think Mum and Dad care what a big, ugly doll says," I replied.

The girls turned and started to leave. "You'll be sorry," Katie warned me. "You'll be sorry you were nasty to Mary-Ellen."

"Mary-Ellen says you'll be sorry," Amanda added. The doll's big head bounced on her shoulder as she walked out of the room.

I slammed the door shut and let out a long sigh. Why do six-year-olds have to be so annoying?

I finished feeding Petey. Then I called a few friends and talked for a while, trying to make plans for the weekend.

I fell asleep around eleven-thirty. I dreamed about my friend Harrison Cohen. I dreamed that he and I could fly. We were flying over our school, and all our friends were amazed.

A sharp *CLICK* pulled me from my dream.

I woke up with a startled gasp. And squinted into the darkness of my room.

I heard another metallic *CLICK*. And then a sharp scraping sound.

A silvery blade flashed in the darkness.

Huh? A blade?

What's going on? I wondered.

I tried to move. Too late.

The blade swooped down to my throat — and I started to scream.

I shot out both hands. I tried to grab the blade. Push it away.

I heard a soft giggle.

The bedside light flickered on.

"Huh?" I let out a shocked cry as I stared at my sisters' grinning faces.

Katie held a pair of long metal scissors in her hand. Her smile faded. "You ruined our surprise," she moaned.

"Huh? Surprise?" My heart pounded in my chest. "What are you *doing* in here?" I cried breathlessly.

"We wanted to surprise you," Katie replied. "We wanted to give you a haircut."

My mouth dropped open — but no sound came out. I was too horrified to speak.

"A *haircut*?" I finally choked out. "A *haircut*?"

"Why did you have to wake up?" Amanda cried. "You ruined everything!"

"I — I'll ruin *you*!" I cried. With a furious

5

shriek, I grabbed the scissors from Katie's hand.

The girls are always playing horrid tricks on me. But never anything as horrible as this. "Whatever gave you the idea —?" I sputtered.

"Mary-Ellen said you need a haircut," Katie replied, tugging my hair. "It was Mary-Ellen's idea."

I angrily shoved her hand away. "Get . . . out . . . of . . . my . . . room," I said through gritted teeth. "I will pay you back for this. I promise I will pay you back."

They both sighed and turned to leave.

"Know what I'm going to do?" I called after them. "I'm going to give *Mary-Ellen* a haircut. I'm going to *cut off her head!*"

"Mary-Ellen heard that," Katie replied.

"You'll be sorry," Amanda added.

They slipped back to their room down the hall. It took me hours to get back to sleep. "Maybe I *will* cut the doll's head off," I told myself. "It certainly would improve her looks. . ."

On Saturday afternoon, I was up in my room, waiting for my friend Harrison to show up. Bright sunlight streamed in through the open window. A pretty autumn day.

"Jillian — it's time to go!" I heard Amanda call from out in the hall.

"Yes! Time to go! Time to go!" Katie and Amanda began to chant. "Time to go! Time to go!"

Why do six-year-olds like to chant everything?

"Hey — give me a break!" I held my hands over my ears.

I ignored their cries and gazed into the mirror. I have straight black hair and round green eyes. I'm tall and very thin. I'm the tallest girl in the sixth grade. Sometimes Dad calls me Noodle because I'm so thin and straight.

Guess how much I like that.

The twins are tall and thin and dark-haired too. Katie pulls her hair back in a pony-tail. Amanda usually lets her hair hang over her shoulders.

But I still have trouble telling them apart. Until they talk. Katie is the one with the squeaky voice. She is the crazy one. She is always wired!

Amanda is usually a lot cooler, a lot calmer, a lot quieter and more thoughtful.

Except for now. They were both tugging at me, pulling me to the door, chanting, "Time to go! Time to go!"

"Go where?" I cried.

Mum swept into the room, carrying a pile of clean T-shirts. She set them down on my bed, then made a face at Petey. She hates him too.

"Jillian, have you forgotten about taking your sisters to the Little Theatre?" she demanded.

"Oh, no!" I wailed. "I *had* forgotten!"

Weeks ago, I'd promised the twins I'd take them to see the ventriloquist show at the Saturday matinee.

"You *have* to take us!" Katie squeaked. She tugged my arm so hard, my shoulder cracked.

"You *have* to!" Amanda repeated.

"But I'm meeting Harrison," I protested to Mum. Harrison lives down the block. We've been best friends ever since I made him eat a whole bowl of mud in first grade.

That was five years ago. So far, Harrison hasn't done anything to pay me back. I think he's waiting for the right moment.

Mum squinted hard at me. Her no-nonsense look. "You promised them, and you are taking them — now!" she ordered.

The twins exploded in a deafening cheer.

"Take Harrison with you," Mum added. "I'm sure he'll enjoy the show."

Yeah. Of course. About as much as eating mud.

Mum squinted at me even harder. "Jillian, you want to make money entertaining kids at birthday parties — right?"

"Right," I replied.

"So maybe you'll get some good ideas at this show," Mum said.

I groaned. "Mum — I want to be a clown. Not a stupid ventriloquist."

Mum leant close to me. "You promised them," she whispered.

"Okay, okay. We're going," I said.

The twins cheered again.

"Actually, Harrison likes this kind of stuff," I added. "He'll probably think the show is amazing."

"If Harrison is coming, then Mary-Ellen has to come too!" Katie cried.

"Yes!" Amanda agreed. "Mary-Ellen wants to see the ventriloquist."

"No way!" I protested. "There's no way I'm taking that big, ugly monster!"

Amanda disappeared across the hall into the room she and Katie share. A few seconds later, she was back, dragging the big doll. "Mary-Ellen says she has to come with us!"

"But — but —" I sputtered. "She's too big. I'll have to buy a ticket for her. She will have to have her own seat!"

"I'll hold her in my lap!" Katie cried.

"No. *I'll* hold her!" Amanda insisted.

"I'm not taking her," I insisted. I glanced at the clock on the mantelpiece. "Put the doll down and let's go," I said. I picked up my bag.

Amanda didn't move. She hugged the big doll. "I'm not going unless Mary-Ellen goes too!"

"I'm not going, either," Katie croaked in her scratchy voice.

"Okay, okay," I sighed. I could see that I wasn't going to win this argument. "You can bring the doll."

They both cheered. They love winning. And since they are spoilt brats and almost always win, they have a lot of practice cheering.

A deafening sound — a shrill whine — blared through the room. "What is *that*?" I cried.

"You know. It's your dad," Mum replied.

Another shrill whine made me cover my ears.

"He's down in his workshop." Mum sighed. "Still sawing away at that coffee table."

"He's been building that table for six months," I said.

"I'm sure it will be beautiful when it's finished." Mum glanced at the clock. "You're really going to be late."

"Come on, you two," I said. "Let's go and see this show."

"Mary-Ellen too!" Katie reminded me.

"I know. I know," I groaned.

She swung the big doll around. Her heavy plastic hand slapped me in the face. "Hey —!" I cried out angrily.

"Mary-Ellen did it. Not me!" Katie insisted. She stuck out her tongue at me.

Harrison was just walking up the driveway. He's very big. Not chubby. Just *biiig*. Big head, big chest, big, muscular arms and legs. He has a round face, dark, serious eyes and short dark hair.

"What's up?" he called.

"We're going to a ventriloquist show," I told him. "All of us."

"Cool," he replied.

I knew he'd like it.

I thought I'd be bored to tears.

And I was right about that. But here's what I didn't know.

I didn't know this show would ruin our lives.

"When does it start? When does it start?" The twins bounced in their seats. Mary-Ellen bounced on Katie's lap. She swung to the side, and I got a mouthful of frizzy doll's hair.

We had great seats in the centre of the third row. I gazed round. The Little Theatre used to be an old cinema. Now it's used mainly for kids' plays.

The wide stage rose above us with its faded red curtain. The old cinema had had two balconies at the back. But now they're closed off. The rest of the seats are either torn or broken. But the kids didn't seem to mind.

Hundreds of little kids jammed the theatre. They were all shouting and bouncing up and down, like Katie and Amanda, eager for the show to start.

A few rows behind us, a little red-haired girl was crying her eyes out. A boy in a bright yellow sweater was being dragged up the aisle by his mother. She had a handkerchief pressed against his nose, trying to stop a nosebleed.

I turned to Harrison. "Wow. Fun, huh?" I said, rolling my eyes.

He grinned at me. "I think ventriloquists are cool."

Harrison is a weird boy. He never complains. He thinks *everything* is cool.

Sometimes I think he's from the moon.

I felt something bounce off my neck. I spun round. The twins were throwing popcorn at each other. "You're wasting all your popcorn," I told them.

"Mary-Ellen wants her own bag," Katie insisted. "Go and buy a bag for Mary-Ellen."

"No way," I replied. "You can share with her."

"When does the show start? I'm bored," Amanda whined.

"Mary-Ellen is bored too," Katie added.

I ignored them and turned to Harrison. "Remember about next Saturday night?" I asked him.

He squinted his round dark eyes at me. "Huh?"

"Hel-lo!" I knocked on his head. "Anyone in there? We've talked about it a hundred times, remember? How you're going to help me entertain at the birthday party?"

"Oh. Yeah." He scratched his short hair. "We're clowns, right?"

"We have to practise our act," I told him. "I want to be really funny. It's my first job. And Mrs Henly is paying me thirty dollars."

"Paying *us* thirty dollars," Harrison corrected me.

"We don't have enough popcorn!" Katie interrupted. "Mary-Ellen needs her own bag. Go and get it, Jillian. Hurry!" She pushed the big doll in my face.

I couldn't take any more. I lost it.

"Get that ugly thing away from me!" I shrieked. I slapped Mary-Ellen across the face. The doll's head snapped back.

Startled, Katie pulled the doll down into her lap. She sneered at me and stuck out her tongue.

Music blared from the loudspeakers. "Boys and girls, ladies and gentlemen!" a deep voice boomed. "Please welcome Jimmy O'James and his good friend Slappy!"

The music swelled, and the kids all clapped and cheered. Grinning and bowing, the ventriloquist walked out in front of the red curtain, carrying his dummy on his arm.

Jimmy O'James dropped down on the tall stool in the centre of the stage. He was young. He didn't look much older than the teenage babysitters we get for the twins.

Big and broad-shouldered, he wore a black turtleneck sweater over black trousers. He had short brown hair, and a big smile that appeared to be frozen on his face. He never stopped smiling!

Slappy, the dummy, also had a smile that didn't quit. His round blue eyes slid rapidly from side to side, as if he was checking the audience.

Slappy had a wave of brown hair that stood straight up on his head. He was dressed in a red-and-white-checked sports jacket that reminded me of a tablecloth. A white shirt with a red-and-white bow tie. He had baggy grey slacks and black shoes, very big and very shiny.

I glanced at the twins. They were sitting up alertly, silent at last, staring up at the stage. Mary-Ellen was perched on Katie's lap.

"Hello, everyone," the ventriloquist began. "I want you to meet my friend Slappy."

Slappy's red-painted mouth slid up and down. "Are we friends?" he asked. He had a shrill, little-boy voice. "Are we really friends, Jimmy?"

"Of course we are," the ventriloquist replied. "You and I are *best* friends, Slappy."

"Then would you do a best friend a favour?" Slappy asked sweetly.

"Of course," Jimmy replied. "What favour?"

"Could you take your hand out of my back?" Slappy growled.

The kids in the audience laughed. I saw Harrison laughing too.

"I'm afraid I can't do that," Jimmy said. "You see, you and I are *very close* friends."

Slappy tilted his head. "Very close friends? How close? Can you give me a kiss?"

"I don't think so," Jimmy replied.

"Why not?" Slappy demanded in a tiny voice.

"I don't want to get splinters!" Jimmy declared.

The kids all laughed. Katie and Amanda thought that was very funny.

Suddenly, Slappy's voice changed. "You don't want to kiss me? Well, I don't want to kiss you, either. Here's a riddle for you, Jimmy," he growled. His voice came out gruff and hoarse. "What's the difference between a skunk and your breath?"

"I — I don't know," Jimmy stammered.

"*I don't know, either!*" Slappy barked.

The kids in the audience laughed. But I saw Jimmy's smile fade. From our third-row seats, I could see beads of sweat form on his forehead.

"Slappy — be nice," he scolded. "You promised me you wouldn't do that."

"Here's another riddle for you, Jimmy," the dummy growled.

"No, please. No more riddles," the ventriloquist pleaded. He suddenly looked really upset. I knew it was all an act. But why was Jimmy O'James pretending to be so nervous?

16

"What do your face and a plate of creamed corn have in common?" Slappy asked.

"I — I don't like this riddle," Jimmy protested. He forced his smile back. He turned to the audience. "Hey, kids — tell Slappy —"

"What do your face and a plate of creamed corn have in common?" Slappy rasped.

The ventriloquist sighed. "I don't know. What?"

"They both look like vomit!" Slappy screamed.

Everyone laughed.

Jimmy O'James laughed too. But I saw more sweat pour down his forehead. "Very funny, Slappy. But — no more insults. Be nice — or I'll have a new job for you."

"New job?" Slappy asked. "What new job?"

"I'll get you a job as a crash test dummy."

"Ha-ha. Remind me to laugh," Slappy growled. "You're about as funny as stomach cramps."

"Slappy — please. Give me a break," Jimmy pleaded.

Suddenly, Slappy turned sweet again. "Want to hear a compliment?" he asked. "Can I give you a compliment, Jimmy?"

The ventriloquist nodded. "A compliment? Yes. That's better. Let's hear it."

"YOU STINK!" Slappy shrieked.

Jimmy looked hurt. "That's not a compliment," he said.

"I know. I lied!" Slappy exclaimed. He threw back his head and opened his mouth in a scornful laugh.

Katie and Amanda were on the edge of their seats, leaning over the seats in front of them, laughing. I turned and saw that Harrison was laughing too.

"This man is really funny," Harrison said. "That dummy has a *baaad* attitude!"

"Yeah. I suppose so," I replied.

"You can't even see the ventriloquist's lips move," Harrison said. "He's pretty amazing."

"Jimmy, you should be on the dollar bill," Slappy was saying. "Because your face is all green and wrinkled!"

The twins laughed and slapped the seats in front of them.

"Or maybe you should be on the penny!" Slappy screamed. "Know why? Know why? *Because you're practically worthless!* You're worthless, Jimmy! Worthless!"

Sweat poured down Jimmy O'James's forehead. He clenched his teeth and shut his eyes as the dummy screamed at him.

Why does Jimmy look so unhappy, so upset? I wondered.

Why does he look so *afraid*?

"Let's stop the insults and talk to some of the kids," Jimmy suggested to the dummy. "You'll be nice to the kids — won't you?"

"Of course," Slappy replied. "I'm a nice guy."

The ventriloquist stood up and leant over the front of the stage. "Who would like to come up and meet Slappy?"

Dozens of hands shot up. Before I realized what was happening, Katie and Amanda were pushing to the aisle. Then they went running on to the stage. Katie dragged Mary-Ellen with her.

"Oh, wow," I murmured. "This should be interesting. . ."

"That doll is almost as big as you are!" Jimmy O'James exclaimed.

Slappy leant down towards Mary-Ellen. "You're pretty," he told the doll. "Pretty ugly!"

The audience laughed hard. My little sisters

didn't laugh. Katie struggled to hold up the big doll.

"So you're twins, huh?" Slappy growled. "What do you call yourselves — *The Gruesome Twosome*?"

Slappy threw back his head and let out a high-pitched giggle. A few kids in the audience laughed. But most of them didn't think that was funny.

"I bet you share *everything,* don't you?" Slappy said to my sisters. "Which one of you is using the *brain* today?"

Slappy laughed again. Jimmy grabbed him with both hands and shook him. "Stop it, Slappy!" he screamed angrily. "Stop insulting the kids!"

"They love it!" Slappy declared. "They love me — and hate you!"

I leant forward, my heart pounding. Katie and Amanda looked really unhappy. Why was the ventriloquist making Slappy say those nasty things to them?

Beside me, Harrison was laughing hard. "This man is a riot!" he declared.

"I don't think it's very funny," I confessed.

"Girls, I think you're a lot like Niagara Falls," Slappy growled.

Katie and Amanda exchanged confused glances.

"Slappy, you say they're like Niagara Falls,

20

the waterfall?" Jimmy asked. "Why do you say that?"

"They're both big drips!" Slappy cried.

"That's not very nice!" Katie protested.

The audience grew silent.

"Girls, I think you'd better go back to your seats," Jimmy O'James said, shaking his head. "Slappy isn't in a very good mood today."

The girls turned and hurried off the stage. Katie tripped and nearly dropped Mary-Ellen.

"Get your doll a flea collar!" Slappy called after them.

The girls pushed their way back through the row and plopped into their seats. Katie scowled angrily. Amanda shook her head. I could see she was blushing.

Katie leant over to talk to me. "That was really nasty," she whispered.

"He wasn't funny," Amanda added. I could see teardrops form in the corners of her eyes. "I — I was so embarrassed."

"I wasn't embarrassed. I was just angry," Katie whispered.

Two teardrops rolled down Amanda's cheeks. Katie never cries. But Amanda cries if you look at her funny.

"That's just his act," I told them. "Some people think insults are funny. If I was up there and Slappy said those things about *me*, you'd laugh your heads off!"

21

They didn't reply. They settled back in their chairs, and we watched the rest of the show. Amanda stared up at the stage, frowning, her arms crossed over her chest. Katie hugged Mary-Ellen tightly. Neither girl smiled once.

Harrison was the only one who seemed to enjoy the show. "Being a ventriloquist looks like fun," he told me. "You get to say horrible things to people — and everyone blames the dummy!"

The ventriloquist finished his act with a song. He sang one line, and then Slappy sang the other.

"Let's all show our appreciation for Jimmy O'James and his funny friend Slappy!" a voice boomed from off-stage.

Everyone clapped and cheered. Everyone but Katie and Amanda.

Then we started to make our way along the row to the aisle. Katie and Amanda led the way. "Sorry you didn't enjoy the show," I said to them.

"We're going to tell that ventriloquist he's nasty," Katie declared.

"Excuse me?" It was so noisy in the big theatre, I wasn't sure I'd heard her correctly.

"We're going to tell him he shouldn't do that to kids," Amanda said.

"He isn't funny at all," Katie complained. "And we think he should say he's sorry."

"No, wait —" I started.

They pushed their way into the crowded aisle. Everyone was heading for the exits. The girls turned the other way and scooted towards the stage.

"Wait —!" I cried. "I don't think that's a good idea! Hey — Katie? Amanda? Come back!"

Too late. I saw them pull open a little door at the side of the stage and disappear behind it.

I stopped short. Harrison bumped right into me.

"Ow!" He's so big. It was like being bumped into by an elephant.

"Sorry," he muttered. "Where did your sisters go?"

I pointed to the door beside the stage.

"But everyone is leaving!" he cried.

"They want to talk to the ventriloquist," I told him. I had to shout over the loud voices of the kids. Two little boys scooted in front of me, making karate chops at each other as they ran.

I grabbed the sleeve of Harrison's T-shirt. "Come on. Help me find them," I said.

I tugged him to the door and pulled it open. We both tried to go through at once — and got jammed together in the doorway.

"Haven't you had *enough* comedy for one day?" I wailed.

He stepped back, and I moved through the doorway. We found ourselves in a long, narrow hallway. I squinted into the darkness, but I could barely see a thing.

"Weird," Harrison muttered. His voice echoed off the concrete walls. "It's like a tunnel. Are you sure that was the stage door?"

"How should I know?" I snapped. "I just know the girls went in here."

We started walking into the hall. I trailed one hand along the wall. Harrison stayed close beside me.

"Where are they?" I cried. My voice echoed. "They couldn't have gone far."

"Hey — Katie? Amanda?" Harrison called.

We stopped and listened. No reply.

"They're *always* doing this to me!" I declared through gritted teeth. "Remember when they disappeared after the circus? I was so worried. I was so scared they were lost or hurt or something. I searched and searched for them. And they were hiding in the wooden stands, watching me the whole time!"

"Katie? Amanda?" Harrison's voice boomed down the long, dark hallway.

Silence.

"Why don't they have any lights back here?" Harrison demanded. "If this is the stage door . . ."

25

"YAAAIIIII!" I let out a scream as something soft and scratchy wrapped around my arm.

Harrison spun round. "Jillian — what is it?" he cried.

I shook my hand hard. I scraped at it with my other hand.

"A — a spider's web!" I choked out. "Yuck. As thick as a sheet." I struggled to pull it off me. "Ohhh." I uttered a low moan. My whole body prickled and itched.

"This can't be the stage entrance," Harrison muttered.

"Katie? Amanda?" I shrieked. "They're probably hiding," I told Harrison. "I'm going to *kill* them this time. I really am."

Harrison suddenly grabbed my arm. "Jillian — duck!"

I lowered my head. More cobwebs hung down from the ceiling.

The tunnel curved to the right. We stepped into a wash of grey light. I heard voices up ahead.

"Hey —!" I called. "Katie? Amanda? Where are you?"

I heard a girl laugh. But it didn't sound like one of my sisters.

"I think the dressing-rooms must be back here," Harrison said. We passed a door marked STAGE CREW ONLY and then a door with the word PROPS stencilled at the top.

26

I heard a woman yell, "Hurry up."

And then two boys laughed and sang part of a song.

We started to jog. I knew we were getting close.

"Katie? Amanda?" I called. "You'd better not be hiding from me!"

The hall split into two narrower hallways. Harrison and I stopped and stared in both directions. The hall that led to the right was brightly lit. I started to lead the way to it — but then I heard voices in the other hall.

"Let's split up," I said. I pointed to the right. "Take that one. If you find them, drag them to the front of the theatre. I'll meet you there."

I trotted into the hall on the left. "Take no prisoners!" I heard Harrison call. Then he disappeared from sight.

I moved quickly past doors with stars' names stencilled on them. These must be the dressing-rooms, I told myself.

I slowed down when I heard voices up ahead.

"You *promised* me —" a man whined.

Light spilled out from a door opened halfway. I crept up to it.

"You can't *do* that to me!" the man continued. He sounded very angry, very frantic.

"You're blowing hot air on me!" another voice replied. A shrill, tinny voice. *Slappy*'s voice!

I crept up to the half-open door. Keeping myself hidden, I leaned my head forward and peeked inside.

"You ruined everything!" Jimmy O'James cried angrily. He held Slappy on his arm, just as he had on-stage. "You really hurt me. I mean it. You hurt me."

"Your *face* hurts me!" the dummy snarled back.

What's going on here? I wondered. I took a step closer. I leaned into the doorway.

They really seemed to be arguing. But that was impossible!

Why on earth was the ventriloquist doing this?

Jimmy O'James took a long drink from a bottle of water. "I can't let you do this!" he sputtered. "I have to stop it — now."

The dummy let out a low growl. "Stop *this!*" he grunted.

And to my shock, the dummy swung his arm — hard.

His wooden fist slammed against the ventriloquist's face.

Jimmy O'James staggered back. He grabbed his nose. Blood trickled down his chin.

Huh? I gaped in amazement. The dummy had given him a bloody nose!

Something is wrong here, I told myself.

Something is very wrong.

I raised my eyes — and cried out.
Jimmy O'James was staring at the doorway.
He saw me.

The ventriloquist's eyes bulged.

The dummy turned too. Slappy's mouth dropped open. Then his head drooped, and his whole body collapsed.

Jimmy O'James set Slappy down on a table. Then he turned back to me. "I didn't see you there," he said. His dark eyes studied me. He grabbed a tissue off the table and wiped at his bleeding nose.

"He — he *hit* you!" I stammered, pointing at Slappy.

"Huh?" The ventriloquist glanced at Slappy, then shook his head. "No. He didn't hit me. He slipped from my arm, and his hand bumped into me. That's all."

"But — but I saw you *arguing*!" I sputtered.

Jimmy O'James sniggered. "I was just rehearsing. Just practising. I'm doing another show with Slappy tonight." He dabbed at his nose with the tissue.

I felt so confused. "I'm sorry," I said. "I thought —"

"He's just a dummy," the ventriloquist said. "He's not alive."

I gazed at Slappy, folded on the table. He'd looked quite cute on-stage. But now I could see his crooked, painted smile and cold, staring eyes. Even though he smiled, his expression appeared angry, almost cruel.

"I really thought you were fighting with him," I told Jimmy O'James.

He lowered the tissue and smiled. "I suppose that makes me a great ventriloquist!" His smile faded. "Are you lost or something?"

"Oh. No." I suddenly remembered why I had wandered back there. "My sisters ran away," I told him. "They were looking for you. Have you seen them?"

He shook his head. "No. Nobody."

"I'd better find them," I said. "Sorry I bothered you." I turned from the doorway.

"No problem," the ventriloquist called after me.

"No problem," a shrill, hoarse voice — Slappy's voice — repeated.

I found the twins at a water fountain near the toilets at the back of the lobby. I rushed up to them breathlessly. "I've been searching all over for you!" I cried. "What are you doing here?"

31

"Giving Mary-Ellen a drink," Katie replied. She and Amanda held the big doll up to the fountain and squirted water on her face.

"You shouldn't have run away," I scolded.

"We didn't! We walked!" Katie insisted. "We got lost in a long tunnel and ended up here."

I grabbed each of them by an arm. "Come on. Let's go home."

"But Mary-Ellen is still drinking!" Amanda cried.

"And we're not going home," Katie added.

"Excuse me? What do you mean?" I demanded.

"You promised you'd take us for ice-cream," Katie replied. She tossed her pony-tail over her shoulder. "You promised."

"Okay, okay," I muttered. The lobby was nearly empty. The overhead lights were dim. "Have you seen Harrison?" I asked.

"He was talking to some people," Amanda reported. She slung the big doll over her shoulder. The doll's face was dripping wet.

"He probably met some friends," I said. "Come on. Let's go."

I took them to the Dairy Queen on the corner. We had chocolate-vanilla swirl cones. They made me buy one for Mary-Ellen too.

We sat in a booth in the corner, and they pretended to feed it to her. They talked to

Mary-Ellen the whole time and never said a word to me.

Do you understand why I hate that doll? Ever since Dad brought the ugly thing home from a garden sale, the twins have completely ignored me. And they use the doll to drive me crazy!

"Mary-Ellen likes the chocolate better than the vanilla," Katie reported.

I groaned. "Can't we talk about something else? I really don't care what Mary-Ellen likes."

They ignored me and pretended to feed her more ice-cream. I checked my watch. The whole day had been wasted! I had a tonne of home-work to do. And I wanted to call some friends to see what they were doing tonight.

Finally, they finished their cones. They had more ice-cream on their faces than in their stomachs! Mary-Ellen too! It took a whole packet of napkins to get them cleaned up.

Then I practically had to drag them home. They kept stopping and pointing out houses and trees and cars to Mary-Ellen. It took *hours* to walk four blocks!

By the time we reached home, I wanted to tear that doll apart. Tear her apart and stuff her pieces in the bin.

The girls hurried to find Mum. I was so glad

to get away from them. I made my way into the
living-room.

And stopped with a gasp.

Slappy was sitting on the sofa!

I let out a sharp cry.

"How ... how did you get here?" I stammered.

The dummy stared back at me with that crooked smile and those cold eyes.

Then he sniggered. His laugh started softly, then grew louder.

I gasped. This isn't happening, I told myself.

Harrison popped up from behind the sofa. His dark eyes flashed gleefully. He was grinning so hard, I thought his face would break!

"Jillian, did you really think the dummy was laughing?" Harrison demanded.

"No. Of course not!" I lied.

"Then why did you talk to him?" Harrison asked.

I stepped up to the sofa. "Where did you get that thing?" I cried. "What is he doing here?"

"He followed me home." Harrison laughed.

"No. Really," I insisted.

The dummy stared up at me from the sofa. Close up, I could see small cracks in his forehead. His painted hair was chipped. Pieces of the red-brown paint had flaked off.

He had a small chunk of wood missing from his bottom lip. His checked sports jacket was frayed. Two buttons were missing.

"Yuck. He's so ugly," I declared.

"You're cute too!" Slappy shot back.

No. Harrison pretending to be Slappy.

"Stop it," I snapped. "You're not funny. Now answer my question. How did this dummy get here?"

Harrison dropped down on the arm of the sofa. He pushed the dummy, and Slappy fell on to his side.

"At the theatre, I met some kids from school," Harrison began. "They were working on the stage crew. Helping out backstage at the ventriloquist show. I couldn't find your sisters. So I hung out with them for a while."

"So?" I asked. "Then what?" It always takes Harrison *years* to tell a two-minute story!

Harrison picked up the dummy's shiny black shoe. Then he let it fall back to the sofa. "I went looking for you," he continued. "But I couldn't find you. I suppose you'd already left."

"I had to take the girls for ice-cream." I sighed.

"So I talked to my friends some more. Then

I went out of the theatre. Through the back door."

He shifted his weight on the sofa arm. "I headed to the front. There was a whole load of dustbins at the side of the theatre. The lid was off the first bin. And there was Slappy, stuffed in the rubbish."

"But, Harrison, that's impossible!" I cried. "Why would Jimmy O'James throw away his dummy?"

Harrison shrugged. "He probably has a lot of dummies. This one looks pretty old. Maybe he's broken or something."

"Yeah. Maybe . . ." I said.

I reached down to examine him.

And he clamped his jaws down hard on my hand.

"Let go!" I shrieked. "Let go! Harrison — help me! He won't let go!"

37

I tugged my hand back as hard as I could. But the wooden jaws bit into my skin.

"Ow! Help me!" I cried.

I raised my free hand and struggled to pull down the dummy's chin. My trapped hand throbbed with pain.

"I don't *believe* this!" I moaned.

"Stop pulling!" Harrison ordered. "Jillian, stop for a moment."

He reached across me and grabbed the dummy's face with both hands. Then he pulled the mouth open, wide enough for me to slip my hand out.

"I *told* you he was broken," Harrison said.

I shook my hand, trying to shake away the pain. I had deep purple teeth marks where the dummy had bitten me.

"Wow. That was *fierce!*" I declared, examining my hand. "I think I was more surprised than anything. I didn't even *touch* his mouth." I shook my hand some more.

"He's definitely broken," Harrison repeated, staring down at the dummy. He gazed back up at him blankly. His painted mouth hung wide open now.

"Get him *out* of here!" I cried. The skin on the back of my hand was red and raw. It still throbbed with pain. "Owww. That hurt! You have to take him back to the ventriloquist."

"No way!" Harrison protested. He grabbed up the dummy in both hands. "Jimmy O'James threw him in the bin. He doesn't want him any more. I'm keeping him."

"We should ask Jimmy O'James if it's okay," I insisted. "Maybe he threw him away by mistake."

"We don't know where Jimmy lives," Harrison replied.

I reached into the dummy's jacket pocket. "Maybe he left an address or something."

A slip of yellowed paper fluttered out of the pocket and sailed to the sofa. I picked it up and examined it.

"Is it the ventriloquist's address?" Harrison asked.

"No," I told him. "It's weird. It's some kind of foreign words."

Harrison squinted at me. "Can you read them?"

I started to read the strange words on the tiny slip of paper: "*Karru marri odonna —*"

"Jillian — time for dinner!" Mum's voice rang out from the dining-room.

I didn't finish reading the strange words. "Sorry. Got to eat," I told Harrison. I stuffed the slip of paper back into Slappy's jacket pocket.

"Come on, Jillian — before it gets cold!" Mum called.

"Coming!" I shouted.

Harrison was straightening Slappy's bow tie. I noticed he was being very careful to keep his hands away from the dummy's mouth.

"Hey — I have an idea," he said. "Your dad loves repair projects — right? If I leave Slappy here, do you think he might fix him?"

I stared hard at the grinning dummy. "Maybe," I replied. "I could ask him."

"Cool! Thanks, Jillian!" Harrison set Slappy down on the sofa. Then he hurried home.

I stepped into the dining-room — and let out an angry cry. "Not again!"

The twins had propped up Mary-Ellen in the chair beside me. They both giggled. They knew I hated having to sit next to that big, ugly doll at dinner.

"Do we have to have that *thing* at the table?" I asked Mum and Dad.

Dad shrugged. He was busy trying to pull a wooden splinter from his thumb. He refuses to wear work gloves down in his workshop. So he's constantly getting splinters.

"The doll won't get in your way," Mum said to me. "She isn't doing any harm."

"Mary-Ellen doesn't want to sit next to *you*!" Katie declared with a sneer. "Because you *stink*!"

"Katie — stop it!" Mum scolded. "Didn't your sister take you to a show today? You should be nice to her."

"The show stunk too," Amanda muttered.

"Eat your macaroni and cheese before it gets cold," Mum said. I saw that Mary-Ellen had her own plate of macaroni. Mum and Dad are as bad as the twins. Why do they always have to give in to anything Katie and Amanda want?

We all started to eat. I asked Dad if he could fix Harrison's dummy. Dad said he'd take a look at him after he'd finished the coffee table he was building.

Mum asked the twins about the ventriloquist show. But they ignored her. They were busy having a conversation with Mary-Ellen.

When I asked them to pass the salt, they ignored me too. They kept on talking to that doll.

I sighed and turned to Mum. "Can't you stop them from talking to that doll all the time? It's driving me nuts!"

"You talk to your lizard!" Katie accused. "You talk to that gross lizard all the time."

"And Mary-Ellen is nicer than a lizard!" Amanda declared.

"*I just wanted you to pass the salt!*" I screamed.

Katie pressed her hands over her ears. "Stop yelling," she whined. "Mary-Ellen doesn't like yelling."

"That hurt Mary-Ellen's ears," Amanda added. "Apologize to Mary-Ellen, Jillian."

"Yeah. Apologize to Mary-Ellen," Katie insisted.

"AAAAAAGGGH!"

I couldn't take it any more. I let out a scream. Then I grabbed Mary-Ellen's big head — and shoved it down into her plate of macaroni.

After dinner, I carried Slappy up to my room and sat down at my desk to do some homework. But I couldn't concentrate. I felt the dummy's dark, cold eyes on me. And I kept glancing up at his crooked grin.

Finally, I turned the dummy to face the wall. That helped a little. I did some work. Then I called some friends and chatted for a while. Then I went to bed.

But I couldn't sleep. I kept thinking about the twins at dinner and how furious they'd made me. They drove me bananas with that doll.

Then Mum and Dad yelled at *me* for losing my temper.

Was that fair? *I don't think so.*

It's payback time, I decided. Time for a little revenge.

How many nights have I put myself to sleep trying to dream up a good revenge plan?

I sat up. Tonight, I have to do something, I told myself. I suddenly had an idea. It made me chuckle to myself.

Katie and Amanda always keep their trainers by the front door. They slip them on as they head out to school in the morning.

I'm going to sneak downstairs and tie their laces into huge knots, I decided. I sniggered again. I'm a really good knot-tier. I planned to tie so many knots in their trainers, they'd never get them loose. They'd have to cut the laces off with a pair of scissors!

I know, I know. It wasn't the cleverest plan in history. And it wasn't much revenge for all the things they'd done to me.

But it was a start.

I stood up and straightened my nightshirt. Then I crept downstairs in the dark to play my little trick.

I stopped halfway down the stairs. I heard a soft thud. A scraping sound. The squeak of floorboards.

Who is downstairs? I wondered. Are Mum and Dad still up?

I pushed my hair off my forehead. Gripping the banister, I made my way down the rest of the way.

Again, I heard the soft thuds of footsteps and the squeak of the living-room floor.

"Who's there?" I whispered. "Who is down here?"

I squinted into the dark living-room.

And saw two eyes staring back at me. Staring hard without moving, without blinking.

"Who's there?" I repeated, the words catching in my throat.

No reply.

My hand fumbled against the wall until I found the light switch. I clicked on the ceiling light.

And saw Slappy sitting in an armchair, his legs crossed. His hands were folded together in his lap.

"Huh?" My mouth dropped open as I stared across the room at him.

And then he growled, *"Go back to sleep!"*

"Noooo!" I let out a low moan and pressed my hands to my mouth.

The dummy talked!

My heart thudded. The room faded in and out of focus.

The dummy stared coldly at me from his chair.

And then I heard giggling. And a rustling behind the armchair.

"I'm going to *kill* you both!" I cried, my voice still shaky.

Katie and Amanda popped out from behind the chair. They were laughing and congratulating each other and slapping each other high fives.

"Ha-ha. So you fooled me. Big deal," I said, rolling my eyes.

"We scared you to death!" Katie declared.

"You really thought the dummy talked!" Amanda chimed in.

"Maybe I did and maybe I didn't," I scowled. "It wasn't very nice. What's the big idea?"

"Mary-Ellen told us to scare you," Katie replied.

"You pushed Mary-Ellen's face in macaroni, and now she hates you," Amanda declared.

"Well, I hate her too!" I cried. "Hate her! Hate her! Hate her!"

I suppose I completely lost my head. The girls' smiles faded. They suddenly looked frightened. They enjoy playing tricks on me. But they get scared when I go completely ballistic.

"Jillian — can we tell you something?" Katie asked in a tiny voice.

"It's important," Amanda added, her expression solemn now.

"No!" I cried. "No way! No more tricks!"

I grabbed Slappy by the waist and pulled him off the armchair.

The dummy's big wooden head fell back. His eyes gazed up at me. The eyes suddenly looked so real. As if they really could see me.

So real and so cold.

The crooked red lips grinned up at me.

I felt a chill run down my back. Was he smiling like that before?

Why did the expression suddenly seem so *evil*?

"Please? Can we tell you something?" Katie pleaded in a tiny voice.

"It won't take long," Amanda said.

"No. I've had enough of your tricks for one day," I snapped. "Go to bed — now."

I spun away and stormed back upstairs, dragging the dummy with me.

"Please —?" Amanda called.

"Please —?" Katie echoed.

Too bad I didn't listen to them.

At school on Monday, Harrison came running up to me in the cafeteria. "Has your dad fixed Slappy?" he demanded.

"You have peanut butter on your chin," I told him.

He wiped it away with his hand. Then he licked his fingers.

"Gross," I complained. "Why are you doing that?"

He shrugged. "I like peanut butter." He followed me to a table. I set down my tray. Harrison plopped down opposite me. "Has your dad fixed the dummy?"

"Not yet," I told him. "He wants to finish his table first. Then he'll get to the dummy." I sighed. "Slappy is already causing me trouble."

Harrison scratched his dark hair. He broke off a piece of my chocolate chip cookie and stuffed it in his mouth. "What kind of trouble?"

"The twins are already using him to play tricks on me," I told him.

I had two slices of pizza on my tray. Harrison picked up a slice and started to chew.

"Help yourself," I said sarcastically.

"Your sisters are evil," he said, biting off a chunk of crust.

I rolled my eyes. "Tell me about it."

"I've been thinking about your revenge," he said, his eyes lighting up. "You know. We should do something to that big, ugly doll they carry around. What's her name? Mary Margaret?"

"Mary-Ellen," I said. I grabbed the other slice before he could take that one too.

"We could remove the doll's head," Harrison continued. He made twisting motions with both hands. "And fill it full of worms. Then sew it back on."

"Not gross enough," I replied. "I'd like to smear that doll with cheese and feed it to a bunch of rats."

"That's too kind!" Harrison laughed. "What if we fill the doll with water? Or cut off all her ratty hair and tell the twins she just went bald?"

"Not nasty enough," I said.

Harrison finished the pizza slice. "Is this all you've got for lunch?" he demanded. "I'm still hungry."

I was still thinking about cruel things to do to Mary-Ellen. But I decided to change the subject. "Harrison, do you remember where we are going after school?"

His mouth dropped open. "You and me?"

I nodded. "We're going to the magic shop — remember? We're going to buy some magic tricks to use in our clown act on Saturday night."

He made a disgusted face. "Yeah. Right," he muttered, resting his chin in his hand. "Our clown act."

"You promised!" I cried. "It's my first birthday party — and you promised you'd help out."

"I really don't want to be a clown," he complained. "I don't think I'm funny."

"You're funny," I told him. "Funny-looking."

He didn't smile. "Is that one of the jokes you're going to use at the party?" he asked glumly.

"We have to practise," I said. "So we'll be funny. We'll buy a load of funny tricks at the shop. The kids will like that."

Harrison sighed. "Remind me why I'm doing this?"

"Because you're my friend," I replied.

"No. What's the *real* reason?" he demanded.

"Because Mrs Henly is paying me thirty dollars — and I'm giving you half of it."

"Oh. Right," Harrison said, snapping his fingers. "Now I remember."

After school, we rode our bikes to the magic shop. It's a tiny shop that also sells comic books and greeting cards and T-shirts.

Harrison and I leant our bikes against the wall at the side of the building. Above us a red-and-yellow sign proclaimed: THE MAGIC PLACE.

Heavy grey clouds rolled over the sun. A dark shadow swept over us as we walked to the front.

"Wait up!" Harrison stopped and squatted down to tie one of his trainers' shoelaces.

I turned the corner — and gasped.

The ventriloquist! Jimmy O'James!

I recognized him instantly in his black turtle-neck shirt and black jeans. He carried a MAGIC PLACE shopping bag. He was two or three shops away, heading for the car park.

"Hey —!" I called. "Hi!" I waved at him frantically.

He turned and narrowed his eyes at me.

"We have your dummy!" I shouted. "We have Slappy!"

The ventriloquist's expression changed. I saw his mouth drop open and his eyes go wide. "Get rid of him! Please!" he cried. "Get rid of him — before it's too late!"

51

"Huh? What do you mean?" I cried.

"Jillian —?" Harrison came trotting around the side of the building. I turned back to him. "It's the ventriloquist!" I told him. "He's here! He —"

Harrison gazed past me. "Where?"

I spun back. The ventriloquist had vanished.

"He's gone," I murmured, shaking my head. "I told him we had Slappy. And he said to get rid of him. Get rid of him before it's too late."

Harrison twisted up his face. "What's that supposed to mean? What's his problem?"

I shrugged. "How should I know?"

"He's weird," Harrison said. "He didn't tell you to give him back — did he?"

"Well . . . no," I replied.

"Good. We're keeping him." Harrison pulled open the door to the shop. We both tried to go in at the same time — and jammed together in the doorway.

52

"Always a comedy act," I muttered.

Harrison grinned. "Maybe we should do that in our clown costumes on Saturday night. You know. Get stuck in a doorway?"

"Keep thinking," I told him.

The shop was empty except for a couple of kids pawing through a stack of old comic books. The magic tricks were at the back.

Harrison and I made our way to the shelves of tricks and gazed at the boxes. THE DISAPPEAR-ING DOLLAR. THE ENDLESS HANDKERCHIEF. THE LIVING TOP HAT.

"These are real magician tricks," Harrison said, picking up a box. "These aren't kids' toys."

"I know," I replied. "We want to be pros — don't we? We want to impress the kids."

"But maybe these are too hard." Harrison snapped his fingers. "Know what would be better? Balloon animals. We could do a balloon animal for each kid."

I frowned at him. "Do we know how to make balloon animals?"

"Well . . . not exactly."

"I think magic is probably easier," I said. "Besides, balloon animals are a bit babyish."

"How old are these kids?" Harrison asked.

"Four," I replied. I picked up a box: SQUIRTING PLAYING CARDS. "This looks like fun," I said, holding it up to Harrison. "We could pretend to

53

play a card game and squirt each other in the face. The kids would like that."

"How about this one?" He pulled another box off the shelf. REALISTIC GUILLOTINE. "The kid puts his head under the blade and —"

"I don't think so." I pulled out a trick from the bottom shelf. WHIPPED CREAM SURPRISE. "This could be good," I said. "You fill it up with whipped cream. It looks like a pie. But when someone bends down close to it, you squeeze this pump and it squirts the whipped cream in his face."

Harrison laughed. "We'll do an all-squirting act. Squirting stuff is always funny."

"Especially to four-year-olds," I added.

We bought the squirting cards and the squirting pie and a few other tricks. I could see that Harrison had a much better attitude. He was starting to get excited about performing at the party.

Maybe we'll be good, I thought. Maybe this party is just the start.

Maybe we'll become the most popular birthday party clowns in town.

Maybe we'll become RICH birthday party clowns!

I strapped the shopping bag bulging with magic tricks over my handlebars. And the two of us rode home, talking excitedly about our clown act.

I was in a really good mood.

Until I walked into the house.

Until I carried the bag up to my room.

I stepped into my bedroom.

And let out a startled scream.

The bag of tricks fell from my hand. The boxes bounced over the floor.

I stared at Slappy. He was perched on the table beside my glass lizard cage.

The glass lid lay on the floor, cracked in half.

Slappy leaned over the open cage. His head was turned towards me. His mouth hung open in a cruel, mocking grin.

Both of his hands were lowered into the cage, as if he was reaching in for Petey.

And Petey . . .

Where was he?

Where was my lizard?

"What have you done with Petey?" I shrieked.

Leaning over the empty glass cage, the dummy grinned across the room at me.

I dropped to my hands and knees and began frantically searching for the lizard. I crawled from one end of the room to the other, peering under the desk, under my chair, in the wardrobe. I pulled up the bedspread and searched under the bed.

"Petey? Petey —?"

No sign of him.

I climbed to my feet and spun to the bedroom door. It had been wide open when I arrived. Had the lizard crawled into the hall?

I dived out into the hall. Searched up and down.

No lizard.

I heard voices and music down the hall. The TV was on in the twins' room. I jerked open the door. Katie and Amanda were sitting on the floor with Mary-Ellen between them. Watching a cartoon show.

"*Where is he?*" I shrieked. "What did you do with him?"

They spun round, letting out startled cries. Mary-Ellen toppled on to her side.

"What's wrong?" Katie asked, jumping to her feet.

"You *know* what's wrong!" I screamed. "Where is Petey? Where?"

I grabbed Katie by the shoulders and started to shake her.

"Stop it! Stop it!" Amanda tried to pull me away. "We didn't touch Petey! Jillian — stop it!"

"Yes, you did!" I cried. "You little brats are going to pay for this!"

"What's going on?" Dad's voice boomed over the noise from the TV. He was still in his over-coat, still carrying his briefcase. He had just walked in from work. "Jillian — what is the problem?"

"Another one of their nasty tricks!" I screamed, letting go of Katie. "This time, they *killed* my lizard!"

"Huh?" His face filled with surprise. "Killed it?"

"We did not!" Katie and Amanda cried in unison.

"We didn't touch her lizard!" Amanda insisted.

57

"Really, Dad!" Katie added. "She's crazy! Ow! She hurt my arms!" Katie rubbed her shoulders and made a pouty face.

"I'll do worse than that!" I threatened. "Look, Dad."

I dragged him into my room and showed him Slappy and the open, empty cage. The girls came running in. They pretended they hadn't seen any of this before.

"I searched everywhere for Petey," I told Dad. "We've *got* to find him! He can't live very long without food or water."

Dad shook his head sadly. He dropped his briefcase on to my bed and turned to the twins. "You really went too far this time," he told them.

"But we didn't do it!" Katie protested.

"We didn't! We didn't! We didn't!" Amanda chanted.

"Well, the dummy didn't do it," Dad told them sternly. "I don't want any more lies, girls. We tell the truth in this house. I mean it."

Dad turned to me. "Petey has to be somewhere in the house, Jillian. He's slow. He couldn't have gone far. We'll all hunt for him. We'll find him before he starves to death."

"But what if he climbs into a radiator or something?" I wailed. "What if we can't find him?"

Before Dad could answer, Mum came burst-

58

ing into the room. "What's all the fuss about?" she demanded. Her mouth fell open when she saw Slappy perched over the open cage.

"We didn't do it!" Katie squeaked before Mum had a chance to accuse her.

"We didn't!" Amanda insisted.

"Is the lizard okay?" Mum asked.

"We don't know. He's gone!" I cried.

Mum shook her head at the twins. "You've done a really terrible thing this time, girls."

"Why won't anyone believe us?" Katie screamed.

Dad put a firm hand on each of the twins' shoulders. "Enough talk. We can discuss this later. Now let's each take a different room — and search."

Katie crossed her arms in front of her chest and pouted. "I won't search until you say you believe Amanda and me," she declared.

"No!" Dad replied sharply. "We *don't* believe you, Katie. There's no way that a dummy can climb up on a table by itself and — and — oh, *no!*"

We all saw it.

We all saw Slappy start to move.

We saw his head tilt back. And then we saw his mouth open.

All five of us froze — and stared in shock as the dummy moved on his own.

"Whoa." I grabbed Dad's arm.

The twins both uttered frightened cries.

Slappy's head tilted. His mouth opened wider.

And Petey poked out from between the dummy's lips.

"Huh?" I let out a gasp. I let go of Dad's arm and went running across the room.

The lizard slid his front legs out over Slappy's chin. His head moved from side to side, as if he was glancing around the room.

"Petey — how did you get in there?" I cried.

I gently pulled the lizard the rest of the way out of the dummy. Slappy fell heavily off the table and landed on the floor at my feet. I cradled Petey tenderly in my hands and turned back to Mum and Dad.

"He's okay," I reported.

My parents were both still frozen in shock. Finally, Mum opened her lips and let out a long whoosh of air. "Wheeeewww. Glad that's over."

Dad laughed and scratched his bald spot. "I really thought the dummy was moving!" he exclaimed. "What a scare!"

The twins were huddled by my bed. "We didn't do it," Amanda said softly. "Really, Jillian."

"Of *course* you did," Mum snapped. She pressed her hands against her waist and glared angrily at them. "There's no one else in this house. I didn't do it. And your father didn't do it. So who does that leave?"

"But — but —" both girls sputtered.

"But we wouldn't try to kill a live animal!" Katie finally choked out.

Mum shook her head. "This was a terrible thing. Not a joke. I want both of you to go and get Mary-Ellen," Mum ordered. "Put the doll away in your wardrobe."

"But Mum —" Katie started.

"Put the doll in the wardrobe," Mum repeated sternly. "You can't bring her out again until you tell the truth about what you did — and apologize to Jillian."

"But Mary-Ellen won't *like* it in the wardrobe!" Katie protested.

"We can't put her away," Amanda insisted. "We can't!"

Mum just stared at her in reply. She turned

61

to me. "Jillian, go and put Mary-Ellen away in their wardrobe. Now."

The girls continued to protest.

I set Petey down carefully in the glass cage. He seemed perfectly fine. I think he probably enjoyed his exciting adventure.

The cage lid was cracked. But it still fitted over the top of the cage. I made sure it was on tight.

Then I made my way into the twins' room. Mary-Ellen was sitting on the floor in front of the TV. I heaved the big doll over my shoulder and started to the wardrobe.

"No! Please!"

Katie and Amanda burst in in front of me. "Please don't put her in there!"

"Mum said," I replied quietly. I jammed the doll on to the top shelf where the girls couldn't reach her. Then I closed the wardrobe door. "If you want her back, just tell the truth," I instructed them.

I hurried back to my room and shut the door. Petey was moving around in the cage. Back to normal.

I shook my head, thinking about Katie and Amanda. They were always pulling nasty tricks on me. They both definitely had a cruel streak.

The haircut in the middle of the night was pretty bad. But this was even worse.

Revenge. The word burst into my mind. I'd

been planning for so long to pay them back for all their cruel tricks.

Now was the time. But what could I do? What would be the perfect revenge?

I tried to imagine them sneaking into my room. Pulling Petey from his cage. Propping Slappy over the cage. And stuffing the lizard into the dummy's mouth.

Hard to believe . . .

And then another picture flashed into my mind.

I pictured myself standing in the dark hall of the Little Theatre, outside Jimmy O'James's dressing-room. Watching the ventriloquist argue with the dummy.

And once again I pictured Slappy swinging his arm and slamming his fist into the ventriloquist's nose.

Impossible, I told myself. That didn't happen.

I gazed down at Slappy, still sprawled on my bedroom floor. His dark eyes stared blankly up at me.

I felt a chill.

"I'm putting you away too," I told him.

I bent down to pick the dummy up — and once again, his jaws snapped down on my hand.

"Oww!" I let out a cry. And struggled to prise my hand loose.

He isn't biting me, I told myself.

The jaws are just stuck. Just stuck . . .

I slapped the knees of my baggy, polka-dot costume and laughed. "You look *amazing!*"

Harrison growled at me. He scratched the ball of red hair on the top of his bald head. His face was white except for the big, painted black mouth that swept from one big rubber ear to the other. His eyes were also ringed by huge black circles.

"I'll never forgive you for this, Jillian," he said. The blue ruffle around his neck bobbed up and down as we walked. "I just hope we don't run into any kids we know."

We made our way up the Henlys' gravel driveway, dragging our bag of tricks with us. I was the happy clown, and Harrison was the sad clown. Mum and Dad had both worked for days on the costumes.

Dad had wanted to build mechanical arms that would pop out from our sides. Mum convinced him we wouldn't be able to move at all with heavy machinery under our costumes.

As we stepped on to the front doorstep, my stomach began to flutter. I could hear kids shouting and laughing inside the house.

I raised my finger to the doorbell. "Hope they like us," I murmured to Harrison.

"If they don't, I'll give them a few shots with this!" Harrison proclaimed. He pulled out the big air horn Dad had given him. The horn was loud enough to blast aeroplanes out of the sky. I don't know why Dad thought we needed it.

I pushed the doorbell again. Again.

The kids were making such a racket inside, no one could hear the bell.

"This will get them," Harrison declared. He pressed the trigger on the air horn. The burst of noise nearly blasted me off the doorstep.

The front door swung open. Mrs Henly smiled out at us. "The clowns have arrived!" she announced.

She's a plump, round-faced woman. She had put her white-blonde hair up on top of her head, but several strands were falling over her forehead. She wiped sweat off her chin.

"Four-year-olds," she said, sighing. "I hope you two can quieten them down. They're going nuts!"

Mrs Henly led us into the living-room. I saw several other parents huddled in a small study.

Harrison and I stopped in the doorway and stared at about twenty little kids, running around the room, jumping on the sofa, bouncing off the walls, hitting each other with gift-wrapping rolls, throwing stuffed toys at each other.

Mrs Henly cupped her hands around her mouth. "The clowns are here!" she shouted. "Everyone sit down for the clown show."

It took a long time, but we finally got them all sitting on the floor. A few of them were still hitting each other, and two boys were arm-wrestling on the sofa. But they were quiet enough for us to start our show.

"I'm Zippy and he's Zappy!" I announced. "We're going to make you laugh! First, we'll take a bow!"

Harrison and I took deep bows and cracked heads, just as we'd practised.

I waited for the kids to laugh. But they didn't.

Harrison and I cracked heads again, just in case they'd missed it. This time, Harrison bowed too fast, and we *really* cracked heads!

The kids stared at us in silence. "When do we get cake?" a red-haired girl asked.

"Sshhh. Watch the show!" Mrs Henly ordered.

"It's *my* birthday! I want cake!" the red-haired girl screamed.

"Zappy and I are going to tell you some funny knock-knock jokes," I announced. "Knock

knock!" I shouted, and I knocked on Harrison's white head.

I thought the little kids would crack up when I knocked on his head. But they stared up at us in silence.

"Knock knock!" I repeated, knocking on him again.

"Who's there?" he asked.

"Harry!"

"Harry who?"

"Harry up and answer the door!"

Silence. A cold silence.

Several kids began to whisper to each other. Two girls near the sofa started a shoving match.

"They don't get the jokes," Harrison whispered. "They're too young." He pointed to the bag. "Start the tricks."

"Okay. Good idea." I pulled out the squirting cards. I knew this would make them laugh.

Harrison and I had practised and practised our squirting card game. Each time we picked a card, we squirted each other in the face.

"They're going to go nuts for this one," I whispered. "Let's play cards, Zappy!" I announced loudly. "Do you kids like to play cards?"

"No!" the birthday girl answered. Several kids laughed. The first laughter we'd heard all afternoon.

"Let me cut the deck!" Harrison declared. He pulled out a huge butcher's knife.

67

"Put that knife away!" Mrs Henly shrieked. A little boy near the fireplace started to cry.

"Sorry. Just a joke," Harrison gulped. He shoved the knife into the bag.

"You're a very bad card player, Zappy," I said, dealing him a card. "When it comes to cards, you're all wet!"

I squeezed the pump hidden in my costume pocket. The card didn't squirt. I squeezed it again.

No water. Nothing.

"Well, here's a card for you!" Harrison cried. He held the card towards my face. I could see him squeezing the hidden pump in his costume.

But the card didn't squirt.

The kids started to become restless. Two girls began chasing each other around the sofa. Three boys started wrestling.

"Did you fill the cards with water?" Harrison whispered.

"Me?" I cried. "*You* were supposed to fill them!"

"No. *You* were, Jillian."

"Is it time for cake *now*?" the birthday girl demanded.

"These clowns are stupid!" the boy next to her griped.

"They stink," a boy grumbled, his head buried in his hands.

"Give them a chance!" Mrs Henly scolded.

My stomach suddenly felt heavy as a rock. My knees were trembling. I knew I was sweating my make-up off.

We were bombing. We hadn't made them laugh once. "They *hate* us!" I whispered to Harrison.

He motioned wildly to the bag. "Get the next trick. Hurry!"

I pulled out the whipped cream pie. My hands were shaking as I unwrapped it.

"It isn't time for birthday cake," I announced. "But who would like to try some birthday *pie*?"

"YAAAY!" Several kids cheered. Several jumped up and down, raising their hands.

"This is yummy pie," I told them.

"What kind?" a pouty-looking, dark-haired girl demanded. "Is it apple? I hate apple."

"It's a whipped cream pie!" I told her. "I need two volunteers to try it. Who wants to try some birthday pie?"

I set the trick pie on the coffee table. Then I called a boy and a girl to the front.

Harrison and I didn't plan to squirt the kids with the whipped cream. We planned to let them sniff the pie. Then Harrison and I would bend over the pie to sniff it — and we'd both get whipped cream in the face!

We hadn't been able to practise this one because the whipped cream had to be added at the last minute. But we knew we *had* to get big laughs with this one.

"Go ahead. Sniff the pie," I urged the boy and girl.

They were really cute. They didn't want to get too close.

"Are you going to push it in our faces?" the little girl asked.

"Would Zappy and I do a thing like that?" I cried. "Go ahead. Just sniff it."

Slowly, they bent down to sniff the pie.

And big, wet globs of whipped cream shot up and splattered their faces.

"Ooops!" Harrison cried.

All around the room, kids gasped in surprise. A few started to laugh.

But the boy and girl let out deafening shrieks.

"My eyes! My eyes! It's burning my eyes!" the boy wailed. He slapped frantically at his face, struggling to wipe the whipped cream away.

"It's burning me!" the girl cried. She began to sob. "Make it stop! It's burning my skin!"

Mrs Henly hurried over. Several other parents came running out of the study. A lot of kids were crying. The boy and girl were screaming at the top of their lungs.

Mrs Henly glared furiously at me. "What have you done to them?" she snapped.

"Must be something wrong with the trick," I explained lamely.

She dragged the kids to the bathroom to wash their faces.

The other parents struggled to calm down the crying kids.

My heart was pounding. I felt sick. "What went wrong?" I asked Harrison.

I stuck my finger in the whipped cream. And took a tiny taste.

"Yuck!" I groaned. "It's not whipped cream!"

"Huh?" Harrison took a tiny taste. "It's soap!" he declared, making a face. "Shaving cream or some kind of soap! No wonder it burned their eyes!"

"I — I filled it before I left home," I stammered. "I don't understand —"

I stopped. Suddenly, I knew what had happened.

The twins. Katie and Amanda.

They had done it again. They'd made a switch while I was getting into my costume.

"I'll *kill* them!" I shrieked.

I felt Mrs Henly's firm hand on my shoulder. She hurried Harrison and me to the door. "You kids need to practise," she said angrily. "I'm going to call your mother, Jillian."

"Huh? Call my mother?" I cried.

"To explain to her why I can't pay you. You've ruined Joslyn's birthday party. You've just ruined it."

She practically shoved us out of the door.

Harrison and I stepped out under dark skies. Cold raindrops hit my face and shoulders. I knew the white clown make-up was running down my face, but I didn't care.

I let out a sob. "What am I going to do?" I wailed. "How can I explain to my mum what happened? I'm so *embarrassed*!"

"Just tell her we stunk," Harrison moaned.

We trudged sadly down to the street. Our trainers crunched over the gravel drive. The wind changed direction, blowing the cold rain into our faces.

Harrison turned to me. His eyes flashed excitedly inside the black make-up circles.

"Jillian, I have an idea!" he cried. "Let's bring Slappy to life!"

I stopped and stared at him. "Have you gone mad? What are you saying?" I cried.

"Let's do a ventriloquist act for our next party on Saturday night," he replied. He heaved the bag to the kerb. "We don't need these stupid tricks, Jillian. Let's work up a funny act with dummies."

"Get serious," I muttered. The rain spattered my head and shoulders. The heavy eye make-up ran into my eyes.

"I *am* serious," Harrison insisted. "You can use Slappy. I'll get another dummy. We'll get a load of joke books and put together an act for them. It'll be great. Better than Jimmy O'James! I mean, *two* dummies *have* to be funnier than one!"

The rain came down harder. I rubbed my eyes, trying to get the make-up out. The white make-up ran down over my clown ruffle. The wet costume stuck to my skin.

"How about it?" Harrison demanded. "A whole new act. What do you say?"

"Well . . . okay," I agreed, rubbing my eyes. "At least we won't need costumes and make-up for a ventriloquist act." I ripped the wet ruffle off and stuffed it in the bag. *I never want to be a clown again!*"

It rained the whole weekend. The weather fitted my gloomy mood perfectly.

When Mum asked me how the birthday party went, I snapped, "Don't even mention it."

Mum probably got the whole ugly story from Mrs Henly, because she never mentioned it to me again.

I cornered the twins in their room and angrily blamed them for ruining my clown act. "You could have blinded those kids with that soap!" I screamed.

"But we didn't do it," Katie insisted. "We didn't touch your stupid tricks."

"We weren't even home," Amanda added. "We were visiting our friend Stevie yesterday — remember?"

I gasped. She was right. The twins hadn't been home.

But then . . . who had switched the soap for the whipped cream?

Who?

*   *   *

74

After school on Monday, I met Harrison. He came pedalling up to me furiously on his bike. "I called the magic shop," he reported. "They don't have a ventriloquist dummy."

I was bent over my bike. The front tyre looked low to me. "So where are you going to get one?" I asked, studying the tyre.

"I called the Little Theatre," Harrison replied. "They gave me the ventriloquist's address."

I squeezed the bike tyre. "Why do you want that?"

"I bet he has another dummy he could sell us," Harrison said. "Or maybe he could lend us one."

I climbed to my feet. "But when I saw him on the street that day, he acted so weirdly — remember? He yelled at me to get rid of Slappy. Then he ran away."

"Maybe he was in a hurry or something," Harrison said. He pulled a sheet of paper from his jacket pocket. "I have his address here. Can you come with me to his house?"

I hesitated. I didn't really want to go and see Jimmy O'James. But I did want to ask him some questions about Slappy. And I didn't want Harrison to go by himself.

"Okay," I said, climbing on to my bike. "What could happen?"

16

"My parents don't like me riding my bike this far," I told Harrison.

He was pedalling hard, holding the ventriloquist's address in one hand. "It's just a few blocks past Dawson, I think," he replied, breathing hard.

We had passed through our neighbourhood, through the town centre, and then through several small neighbourhoods on the other side of town. After some wooded blocks, the houses became smaller and closer together.

"This is a pretty bad neighbourhood," I said as my bike bumped over some railway tracks. A scraggly dog chased us for a few blocks, barking and nipping at my legs.

We pedalled past a row of beat-up-looking mobile homes lined up in a weed-choked plot. "Harrison — are you sure you know where you're going?" I cried.

"Well . . ." He stared at the address in his

hand as if it were a road map. Suddenly, he braked to a squealing stop. "Hey — that must be the house. Up there."

He pointed to a big, grey-shingled house tucked back in the trees. Nearly hidden by low tree branches. The house stood completely dark. A rolled-up newspaper rested on the roof just above the guttering. The lawn was over-grown with tall grass and weeds.

"Yes. This is it." Harrison crinkled up the piece of paper and shoved it into his jeans pocket.

I gazed into the deep shadows of the trees, trying to see the house clearly. "What a creepy house. Doesn't look as if anyone is home," I murmured.

We walked our bikes up the driveway, which was cracked and broken. The tall weeds shifted and rustled as some kind of animal scurried to get out of sight.

A squirrel? A chipmunk?

I shivered.

We set our bikes down on their sides in the tall grass that grew over the front walk. Then we made our way on to the creaking, wooden front porch.

I pressed the doorbell. But I didn't hear it buzz.

Harrison knocked and called out. "Mr O'James — are you home?"

77

We waited, then knocked again. "Anybody home? Hel-lo?"

Harrison knocked one more time — and the front door swung open.

No one standing there.

I poked my head in. Darkness inside. "Anybody home?"

"Let's go in," Harrison urged, giving me a soft push. "Maybe he's in the back or something."

I hesitated. "Go in? Do you think we should?"

"Let's check it out," Harrison said.

"Well . . . okay." I took a deep breath and led the way inside.

A short hallway led into a long, narrow front room. The trees over the house blocked most of the sunlight from the windows. But even in the dim light, I could see that the room was bare.

"Anybody home?" Harrison called, cupping his hands around his mouth. "Mr O'James? Are you here?" His voice echoed off the bare walls.

We made our way quickly to the next room. Movement on the floor made me stop. "Oh, yuck," I moaned.

Cockroaches!

Dozens of them. They scampered over my trainers. I felt them prickling my ankles.

"Owww! Get them off! Get them off me!" I jumped up and down, slapping at the disgusting, swarming bugs.

Then I leapt over them to catch up with

Harrison. "Gross," I muttered. "The place is crawling with bugs."

We found ourselves in a room with a long table down the centre. At first I thought it was the dining-room. But the shelves of tools and supplies on three walls made me realize we were in some kind of workshop.

I tugged Harrison's sleeve. "We really don't belong in here. We should go."

Harrison ignored me and picked something up from a corner of the long table. "Check it out." He pushed it in front of my face.

"Hey —" It was a wooden dummy head. It had the same cold eyes and crooked smile as Slappy's.

"There are body parts all over the room," Harrison reported. He pulled a pair of slender legs off a shelf. Then he picked up another dummy head.

"He must build all of his dummies here," I said, stepping into the next room.

"Maybe he can build one for me," Harrison suggested. "That would be cool."

I poked my head into the kitchen. Bare. No food. No plates or bowls or pots and pans.

"He's gone," I told Harrison. "I think he has moved out."

"No way!" Harrison protested. "We need another dummy."

"Well, it doesn't look as if anyone lives here,"

I said. I made my way into the small dining-room behind the kitchen. "I mean, look around, Harrison. Can you see —"

My words caught in my throat.

I gasped in horror. My hand shot up to my mouth.

Harrison saw it too. "Ohhhh." A sick moan escaped his throat.

We both stared at the dining-room table.

At the human head lying on its side on the table.

Jimmy O'James's head.

We both crept forward, a step at a time. I grabbed Harrison's arm. "Is he —? Is it —?"

Harrison cried out and jerked his arm away. "Sorry," I muttered. I didn't realize how hard I was squeezing his arm.

The ventriloquist's head lay on its left ear. His dark eyes were wide open, staring blankly at the wall.

I swallowed hard as we leaned over the head.

Harrison picked up the head. "A dummy head!" he cried.

"Oh, wow!" I exclaimed. I pressed a hand over my pounding heart, trying to slow it. "I don't believe it! It looks so real! He made a dummy head of himself!"

Harrison used his other hand to move the mouth up and down. "Hello. I'm Jimmy O'James, and I'm a dummy," he said in a hoarse voice, trying not to move his lips.

"Come on. Stop fooling around and let's go,"

I pleaded. "This place is really creeping me out."

"Whoa. Wait," Harrison insisted.

"No. I mean it," I told him. "I'm getting out of here — now!"

"But check this out!" Harrison cried.

I turned to him. He had set the head back on the table. And now he was flipping through a small, tattered book.

"What is that?" I demanded, moving back into the room.

"This is so cool!" Harrison exclaimed. "It's some kind of notebook. A diary, I think."

"Whose diary?" I asked, stepping up to him.

"Jimmy O'James's diary," Harrison replied. His eyes scanned the pages. "Wow. There's all this stuff about Slappy in here."

I pulled the book from Harrison's hands. "Slappy? What about Slappy?"

I quickly skimmed the pages. The diary was written in a tiny, neat handwriting. The blue ink had faded. But it was still easy to read, even in the dim light of the dining-room.

"Wow. This can't be true!" I exclaimed. "The ventriloquist must have been writing a horror book or something. This can't be real."

"Why?" Harrison demanded eagerly. "What does it say?"

"It — it's *unbelievable*!" I stammered. My eyes slid down the page.

"Jillian — what does it say?" Harrison screamed impatiently.

Squinting at the small handwriting, I began to read. . .

> " 'The puppet maker was not a normal man. At least that's what I heard. This is the story as it was told to me. The puppet maker was a sorcerer who used his puppet creations for evil. His puppets and toys made people sick with strange illnesses. He built dolls that injured their owners. Toys that stole precious belongings while their owners slept.
>
> " 'The sorcerer loved spreading misery and evil through innocent-looking toys.' "

"This has to be a made-up story," Harrison interrupted. "It sounds like a story. It *can't* be true."

I chewed my bottom lip. "I don't know," I replied, flipping back through the pages. "I don't know if this is true or not."

I continued reading out loud. . .

> " 'The dummy named Slappy is the sorcerer's most evil invention. He stole a coffin for its wood. He

carved the dummy from the coffin wood.

" 'And then the sorcerer sent his own evil into the dummy. The sorcerer's evil spirit lives inside Slappy, ready to be awakened by the reading of the evil words of magic the sorcerer wrote.

" '<u>The sorcerer's evil lives inside Slappy</u>.'

"These words are underlined in the diary," I told Harrison. I read them again. . .

" '<u>The sorcerer's evil lives inside Slappy</u>.' "

I continued reading. . .

" 'The ancient words of sorcery to bring him alive are written on a slip of paper inside the dummy's jacket. When the ancient words are read aloud, the dummy — and the evil — come to life.

" 'I have managed somehow to put Slappy to sleep. I'm not sure how I did it. I only care that the dummy sleeps. I thew the dummy in the bin, to be hauled away and crushed.

" 'My only hope is that no one finds

him. That no one reads those evil words that will bring him back to life.'"

"Whoa," Harrison murmured, shaking his head. "We found that slip of paper — remember?"

A chill ran down my back. "I started to read those words. Thank goodness I never finished saying them!"

Harrison stared hard at me. "If this story is true, then Slappy really could have come alive. He really could have stuffed your lizard into his mouth."

"And switched the whipped cream in our trick with soap," I added.

We stared at each other in silence.

"But we didn't finish saying the words — remember?" I cried. I took a deep breath. "Besides, this whole story is crazy. Wooden dummies can't come to life — *can* they?"

A loud crash made us both jump.

The sound of the front door slamming.

I closed the little diary. Harrison shoved it into his jeans pocket.

We both froze, staring into the dim grey light.

And listened to slow, scraping footsteps coming nearer . . . nearer . . .

The sound of a dummy dragging itself over the floor.

CLICK, SCRAPE . . . CLICK, SCRAPE. CLICK, SCRAPE . . .

I pictured Slappy, his legs rubbery, his hands dragging along the floor. Pulling himself . . . pulling himself through the house to us.

Harrison and I both gasped as a white-haired man in dark work overalls shuffled into the room. In his right hand, he gripped a cane, which he tapped along the floor. He walked with a limp.

His mouth opened in surprise as he saw us. He leaned heavily on the cane. "What are you kids doing in here?" he demanded. He had a breathless whistle of a voice.

"We . . . uh . . . were looking for Mr O'James," I finally choked out.

The man pointed behind him. "I'm the neighbour," he explained. "I saw the front door open. Thought I'd better see if someone had broken in."

"We thought maybe Mr O'James was home," I told him, glancing at Harrison. "But —"

"He's out on tour," the neighbour interrupted, shaking his head. "A long tour. He just took off. Didn't even say goodbye."

He shifted his cane from hand to hand. "Don't know what the big hurry was. He's an odd bird."

"Thanks for telling us," Harrison said. "Suppose we'd better get going."

A few seconds later, we were back on our bikes, pedalling for home. The sun was dropping behind the trees. We rode into a cold wind.

"*Now* what are we going to do?" Harrison demanded unhappily, pumping hard as we moved uphill. "Where am I going to get a dummy for the birthday party on Saturday night?"

I shifted gears and rolled up beside him. "I have an idea," I said. "*You* can be the dummy. I'll be the ventriloquist, and we can —"

"And I'll sit on your lap and make my mouth go up and down?" Harrison cried. "No way! Forget it, Jillian."

"Well . . . I really don't want to do a ventriloquist act," I confessed.

Harrison narrowed his eyes at me. "Why not?"

"I don't want to use Slappy," I replied. A chill rolled down my back. "I . . . I want to get that dummy out of my house."

Harrison let out a shrill laugh. "You don't really believe what it said in that little book — do you?"

"Maybe," I replied. "Maybe I do. Maybe that dummy really is evil, Harrison. I don't want to mess with it. I —"

"But I've got an amazing idea!" he protested. We braked for a stop sign. "What about Mary-Ellen?" he asked.

I narrowed my eyes at him. "Excuse me? What about Mary-Ellen?"

"Maybe I could borrow that doll from your sisters," Harrison suggested. "She's so big and weird-looking, she'd make a great dummy."

"Well . . ." I stared at him.

"Maybe we could say that Slappy and Mary-Ellen are boyfriend and girlfriend," Harrison continued. "Maybe we could say they're going to get married. That could be funny."

I frowned. "Slappy and Mary-Ellen? You're right. It *could* be funny. But I really don't want to do it. I really don't want to use Slappy."

"Think about it," Harrison pleaded. "It's a great idea, Jillian. And we don't want to be clowns again. Just think about it — okay?"

"Okay," I replied. But I kept picturing Slappy's evil grin. And the words in the little diary repeated in my mind.

It's true, I decided.

The dummy can come alive. The dummy is evil. . .

When I rode up to the house, Mum was waiting for me at the front door. "You're late!" she called as I climbed off my bike and grabbed up my rucksack. "Remember — you're taking care of the twins tonight?"

I'd completely forgotten.

I hurried into the house. "I've put your dinner on the table," Mum said. "Your dad and I have to get going."

"I'll be right down," I told her. "I just want to drop off my rucksack."

I took the stairs two at a time. Burst into my room. Threw the heavy rucksack on to the floor.

I turned back to the door. Stopped. And gasped.

"Oh, nooo," I moaned, staring across the room.

Slappy was sitting on my dressing-table. I saw an open tube of lipstick in his right hand.

Then I read the words scrawled across the mirror in fat red letters:

WHERE IS MY BRIDE?

"Mum! Dad!" I went screaming down the stairs.

They were already out on the front doorstep. Dad was helping Mum with her jacket.

I pushed open the storm door. "I have to tell you —" I started.

Mum turned. "Katie and Amanda are already at the table. Go and make sure they eat a good dinner." She and Dad hurried towards the car in the driveway.

"But Mum —" I cried. "My mirror! You have to see —"

"Tell me later," Mum insisted impatiently. "You've made us very late, Jillian."

"We'll talk to you when we get home," Dad said. He opened the car door and slid behind the wheel.

Mum hurried round to the passenger side. "You're in charge!" she called. "I'm trusting you, Jillian. *I don't want any trouble of any kind.*"

"But — but —" I sputtered.

"One little problem, and all three of you will be grounded for life!" Mum called. She climbed in and slammed the car door.

I stood in the front door, watching the car back down the drive. Pictured the words scrawled in red lipstick on my mirror: WHERE IS MY BRIDE?

When the car turned a corner, I took a deep breath and made my way into the dining-room. Katie and Amanda sat with big bowls of spaghetti in front of them. Katie was twirling a huge knot of spaghetti on her fork. Amanda was picking up long noodles between her fingers.

I stepped up to the table, my heart pounding. "Were you two in my room?" I asked through clenched teeth.

Amanda slurped a long noodle down. Katie looked up at me innocently. "When?" she asked.

"Were you in my room this afternoon?" I demanded in a shaky voice. "Did you put Slappy on my dressing-table? Did you write on my mirror?"

They both squinted at me. "You're crazy," Katie said.

"We didn't go in your stupid room," Amanda added.

This time I believed them.

They were telling the truth. The diary told the truth.

The dummy was alive! Someone had read the words on the little slip of paper.

"I — I'll be right back," I told the girls. "Just sit there and eat your dinner."

I spun away and ran up the stairs to my room.

Perched on my dressing-table, the lipstick tube clenched in his hand, Slappy stared across the room at me.

I grabbed him and lifted him off the dressing-table. I carried him to my bed and set him down on his back.

Then I reached into the jacket pocket where I had stuffed the little slip of paper.

My fingers fumbled in the pocket.

I searched the other pocket.

Then I searched the first pocket again.

Not there. Not there. Not there.

The slip of paper had gone.

Staring down at the grinning dummy, I suddenly put the whole story together. I knew exactly what had happened.

Katie and Amanda were messing around with the dummy. They found the slip of paper. They read the words and brought the dummy to life.

They were terrified. Terrified of what they had done. Too frightened to tell Mum and Dad.

The girls had found out how evil Slappy was. And they knew it was all their fault that he'd come to life. They were too frightened to talk about it. Too frightened they'd get in terrible trouble.

I picked up the dummy in both hands and stared into his round dark eyes. "Is it true?" I cried. "Is it true, Slappy? Did my sisters bring you to life?"

The glassy eyes gazed up at me. The crooked, red mouth appeared to be laughing at me.

"Is it true?" I demanded shrilly. "Is it true?"

I grabbed the dummy by the shoulders and began to shake him. I shook him hard. Harder.

His heavy, wooden head bounced on his shoulders. His arms flew wildly up and down.

I shook him harder. Harder.

Finally, I stopped. I was breathing hard, my heart pounding in my chest.

"I can't let you ruin my life!" I declared breathlessly. "I can't let you destroy our family!"

I heaved him back on to the bed. He bounced twice, then lay still, gazing up blankly, his head tilted, grinning mouth hanging open.

Trying to calm down, I made my way to the top of the stairs. "Are you two eating your dinners?" I shouted.

"Yes. We're eating!" Amanda called up to me from the dining-room.

"Where are you? What are you doing, Jillian?" Katie called.

"I'll be right down," I told them.

I crossed the hall into the bathroom. Leaning over the sink, I threw cold water on my burning-hot face. Then I washed my hands.

I was drying my hands and face with a big bath towel when I heard a crash.

So loud, the house seemed to shake.

Startled, I grabbed the side of the sink. And heard another crash. From downstairs.

I leapt out into the hall.

And heard another crash from downstairs.
And then a horrified cry.
Both twins shrieking and crying.

I dived down the stairs, leaping three at a time.

"Katie? Amanda? What's wrong?" I shrieked.

I burst breathlessly into the dining-room — and cried out in shock.

Slappy sitting at the table?

Slappy?

"How — how did he get down here?" I stammered.

And then my eyes swept over the mess.

Broken dishes. Spaghetti spilled everywhere.

Milk glasses overturned. Red spaghetti stains dripping down the walls and the window curtains. Salad tossed everywhere. A pile of spaghetti on the carpet.

"He did it! He did it!" the twins wailed. They both pointed at Slappy.

The dummy slumped in his chair, head tilted forward. One arm hung at his side. The other hand rested in a puddle of spaghetti sauce on the table.

I gazed from the dummy to the girls, then back to the dummy. "When — ? How —?" I choked out. The words caught in my throat. My legs were trembling so hard, I grabbed the wall to hold myself up.

What a horrible mess. Piles of spaghetti everywhere. And the red stains . . . the shattered dinner dishes.

"He did it! The dummy did it!" Katie cried.

"You've *got* to believe us!" Amanda pleaded.

I *did* believe them.

The dummy slumped lifelessly in the chair. But how did he get down from my room?

My sisters love practical jokes. But they would never go this far.

What could I do? What should I do next?

The phone rang.

I jumped, startled by the sound. Then I spun away from the shrieking girls, away from the dummy, away from the horrible mess, and ran to the living-room to grab the phone.

"Hello?"

"Hi, Jillian. It's me."

"Mum?"

"Is everything okay?" she demanded. "You sound out of breath."

"No!" I cried. "No! Mum — everything *isn't* okay!"

"Huh? What —?"

"The dummy is alive, Mum!" I shouted into

the phone. "You've got to come home! The dummy is alive! He spilled the spaghetti and — and —" I gasped for breath.

"Jillian — stop it!" Mum replied sternly. "Stop it right now. I'm very disappointed in you."

"But Mum —" I desperately wanted to tell her everything. But she cut me off with an exasperated cry.

"Jillian, stop it. I begged you. No more fighting with the twins. You are in charge, Jillian. You have to be the grown-up."

"But — but — Mum —" I sputtered.

"Don't say another word," she insisted. "I'm so disappointed in you. Your father and I will try to get home early. Goodbye."

She hung up.

I swallowed hard. Took a deep breath. And hurried back to the dining-room.

I have to lock up that dummy, I decided. *I have to lock him up before he does any more damage.*

I stopped in the doorway — and stared at an empty chair.

"Where is he?" I cried. "What did you do with Slappy?"

Katie opened her mouth, but no sound came out.

Amanda whimpered and shook her head.

"Where?" I demanded. "Where is the dummy?"

"He — he left!" Katie finally replied in a whisper.

"Excuse me?" I cried.

But then I heard the soft thud of footsteps. A thud and then a scrape. From the front stairs.

"It's *him*," Amanda whispered.

"He's going upstairs," Katie added. She and Amanda exchanged frightened glances.

I froze.

And listened to the *BUMP BUMP BUMP* as the dummy climbed the stairs.

"This can't be happening," I muttered.

I forced myself to move. I flew through the living-room. Then I pulled myself up the stairs.

I stopped in the doorway to my room.

Slappy sat on my bed. He had orange strands of spaghetti on his head and noodles hanging over the shoulders of his sports jacket.

My eyes lowered to the tube of lipstick in his hand.

And then up to the wall above my bed where he had scrawled the words:

WHERE IS MY BRIDE?

"We've all been grounded," I told Harrison. I paced back and forth in my room, balancing the phone between my shoulder and chin. "My parents are so angry, they won't even *speak* to us."

"Bad news," Harrison murmured.

I glanced out of the window. A beautiful, sunny day. No school because of some teachers' conference. But I wouldn't be going anywhere. Or seeing any friends.

"I've never seen them so angry," I told Harrison. "The spaghetti stains won't come out of the curtains or the wall. We've tried everything."

"Did you tell your parents the dummy did it?" Harrison asked.

"They won't listen," I replied. "Every time I mention Slappy, it makes them even more angry. They started *screaming* at me never to mention the dummy again."

"And do you really think he's alive?" he asked.

I shivered. "I *know* he is, Harrison. I locked him in a suitcase. I made sure the suitcase was double-locked. We have to get him out of here. As far away as we can."

"What about the birthday party on Saturday night?" Harrison interrupted. "We need the dummy for the party — remember?" And then he added, "But you're grounded. Does that mean we can't entertain at the party?"

"Mum is going to let me do the party," I told him. "Mrs Simkin called. Her little boy is the birthday boy. But she had a flood in her basement. So we're having the party at my house. Down in the basement."

"So we need Slappy," Harrison declared.

"No way!" I cried. "I told you, I've locked him in a suitcase. I won't let him out. I won't!" I switched the phone to my other ear. "We have to do the clown act, Harrison."

"We can't!" he cried. "Kids *hate* our clown act, Jillian. It was so bad, it made the kids cry — remember?"

"But the dummy —" I started.

"I've written a whole act for the dummy and the doll," Harrison declared. "It's really funny. The kids will love it. We have to do it."

I didn't say a word. I kept picturing the evil grin on Slappy's face as he sat at the dinner table, the dishes broken, spaghetti smeared everywhere. And once again I saw the words crudely scribbled on my mirror and wall: WHERE IS MY BRIDE?

My whole body trembled.

I couldn't do a ventriloquist act with him. I couldn't give Slappy a chance to do more evil.

"Find another dummy," I told Harrison. "That's the only way we can do the act. We can use Mary-Ellen. But I won't use Slappy. You'll have to find another dummy."

"Okay, okay," he agreed. "A new dummy. I'll find one. No problem."

"Give me that!"

"No — it's mine!"

"You said you'd share!"

"Go and get your own!"

The first fight broke out at the birthday party about five minutes after the guests started to arrive.

Six-year-olds can be beasts. I should know. My six-year-old twin sisters are beasts most of the time.

And now, Harrison and I stood together in the centre of my basement rec room, staring at about fifteen six-year-olds, wrestling, hopping, jumping up and down, shouting, laughing, and chasing each other around the room.

Harrison sniggered and shook his head. "Their parents couldn't wait to dump them here and get out."

I sighed. "Can you blame them?"

A balloon burst — and a little girl with red braids started to cry. Harrison hurried to calm her down.

The parents were having their own party next door. Even Mrs Simkin couldn't wait to escape — and it was her son Eddie's party!

"We'll be next door," she said, leaving Harrison and me in charge. "Just shout if you need us."

Harrison finally got the red-haired girl to stop crying. He hurried back to me. A football flew across the room and nearly bounced into the birthday cake. "Mrs Simkin isn't paying us enough!" Harrison sighed.

I glanced across the room. Katie and Amanda appeared to be having a good time. They were showing their huge collection of beanbag dolls to two other girls.

I looked down to see Eddie Simkin, the birthday boy, tugging at my T-shirt. "When does the show start?" he demanded. "We want the show to start."

He began to chant, and a couple of other boys joined in: "We want the show! We want the show!"

"Let's go and get Maxie and Mary-Ellen," I suggested to Harrison. "At least the show will keep the kids quiet for a while."

"Maybe," Harrison said, shaking his head.

Maxie was a goofy-looking, buck-toothed dummy Harrison had found in his uncle's attic. We had practised with Maxie and Mary-Ellen all week, and it had gone really well. In fact, the act was so funny, we'd laughed ourselves silly.

I couldn't *wait* to perform the act for the kids.

We'd hidden Maxie and Mary-Ellen in suit-cases. And we'd stashed them in the cupboard in my dad's workshop on the other side of the basement.

Harrison lifted Mary-Ellen from her suitcase and straightened her hair.

I pulled Maxie's beat-up suitcase from the cupboard and set it on its side.

"Now, don't forget the changes we made in the song," I warned Harrison.

He nodded. "No problem."

I clicked open Maxie's case. And lifted the lid. And reached in for Maxie.

"Noooooo!" A moan of horror burst from my throat.

"How did HE get in here?" I shrieked.

Harrison and I both stared down at Slappy.

Slappy.

Slappy.

Grinning up at us from Maxie's suitcase.

"We want the show! We want the show!"

Across the basement, the kids were all chanting.

"I — I can't do this," I told Harrison. "I'm too afraid."

"We want the show! We want the show!"

Harrison gaped into the suitcase. "Who switched dummies?" he choked out. "How — how —?"

Slappy's grin appeared to spread. His round eyes flashed in the dim basement light.

"We want the show! We want the show!"

Harrison grabbed my arm. "We have to do it," he insisted. "We have to do the show. The kids will riot if we don't. It'll be ugly!"

Behind us, the kids chanted and cheered. They were sitting on the floor, clapping as they chanted, waiting impatiently for us.

"But — he was locked upstairs!" I cried,

staring down at the painted, grinning face. "Locked up tight."

"Just pick him up," Harrison ordered. "We'll do the show. Then we'll get rid of him for good. Pick him up, Jillian. Hold on to him tightly. It'll be okay."

I glanced back at the chanting kids. They were getting restless. I knew Harrison was right. I knew we had to go on with the show.

I took a deep breath — and hoisted Slappy into my arms. Harrison perched Mary-Ellen on his arms. Then we marched across the basement to begin the act.

"It's my birthday!" Eddie declared, pushing his way through several kids. "So I get the best seat." He plopped down right in front of Slappy and me.

Harrison and I sat down on tall, wooden stools. We raised Slappy and Mary-Ellen to our laps. I gripped the dummy as tight as I could. We started our show.

"Hi, doll," I made Slappy say.

"Don't call me doll!" Harrison made Mary-Ellen reply in a high, shrill voice. "I'll slap your face!"

"That's okay with me. Why do you think my name is *Slappy*?" I made the dummy exclaim.

A few kids laughed at that. I glanced down and saw Eddie make a disgusted face.

"You're a blockhead!" Mary-Ellen cried in her high voice. "I'll bet you have termites!"

"You shouldn't call names," Slappy replied.

"Why not?"

"Because that's *my* job!" Slappy exclaimed. "You're too stupid to call names, Mary-Ellen. Do you know the difference between a dead skunk and a peanut butter sandwich?"

"No. What's the difference?"

I made Slappy shake his head. "Remind me never to ask you for a sandwich!"

Several kids laughed at that joke.

But I looked down and saw Eddie still frowning. "That isn't very funny," he called up to me. "Can't you be funnier?"

"*You want funnier?*" Slappy suddenly shouted. "*I'll show you something funnier, kid!*"

I gasped. I hadn't made Slappy say that!

Before I could do anything, the dummy tilted back his head. He opened his jaws wide.

I heard a gurgling sound from deep inside Slappy's stomach.

And then I cried out as the gurgling grew to a roar.

And a thick green liquid poured out of Slappy's open mouth.

It gushed out like water from a fire hose. Thick green gunk. Thick as pea soup.

Slappy turned his head and sprayed the green goo over the kids. It splattered Eddie

Simkin at my feet. Splashed over the walls, the floor. Sprayed over the other kids.

"Ohhhhhh. The smell!" a girl cried.

A foul, putrid odour rose up all around.

Slappy tilted his head back further. Turned. The disgusting green liquid spewed over everyone.

Kids squealed and cried out in disgust. I saw a boy stand up and try to run. But his feet slid in the green gunk, and he toppled back to the floor, face down in the goo.

"It's in my eyes!" a boy screamed. "It's burning my eyes!"

"Ohhhhhh." Moans of horror and disgust rose up over the basement.

I tried to slap my hand over the dummy's mouth to stop the spray.

But Slappy jerked away from me. I cried out as he slid off my lap. He dropped to the floor. Stood on two feet. Tilted up his head and spewed out more of the stinking, thick liquid.

Kids were trying to scramble away. Some were crying. I saw two boys bent over, vomiting on the floor.

I turned to Harrison. "What are we going to do?"

But before Harrison could answer, Slappy took two steps across the floor. He grabbed Eddie Simkin with both wooden hands.

And with surprising strength, Slappy dragged the terrified boy across the room.

"Slappy — stop!" I choked out.

He turned to me, his evil grin wider than ever. His eyes ablaze with excitement.

"This is MY party now!" Slappy screamed. *"I want my bride!"*

"He's *hurting* me!" Eddie shrieked. "Get him off! Get him off!"

"*Keep away from me!*" Slappy barked. "*I'll hurt him! I'll hurt him BAD!*" He jerked Eddie hard, yanking him across the floor.

I froze in horror. Kids were screaming and crying, slipping and falling in the sickening green gunk.

This can't be happening! I told myself.

I turned to Harrison. His hair was soaked in the green liquid. It had splashed over his shirt and jeans.

"What can we do?" I cried over the screams of the kids.

He gave me a helpless shrug.

"I'm going for help!" I told him. I took off towards the basement stairs.

"*Where do you think you're going?*" Slappy demanded angrily. He jerked Eddie from side to side.

"Ow! You're *hurting* me!" Eddie wailed.

My trainers slid in the green goo. I raised both arms. Caught my balance. Started to run again.

I didn't see Slappy's foot jerk up. He tripped me, and I fell forward.

"Ohhhhh!" I let out a cry of disgust as I went face down in the stinking liquid. I slid along on my stomach a metre or so. Rolled on to my side. Pulled myself to my feet.

I wiped the green gunk off my face. I was covered in it.

"If you go upstairs, I'll hurt them all!" Slappy rasped. His shrill voice sent chills down my back.

I slid to a stop and spun round. "Don't touch *any* of them!" I screamed.

"Let me go! Let me go!" Eddie squirmed and struggled to break free. But the dummy's wooden hands clamped harder on the boy's shoulders.

Slappy's evil grin grew wider. His round eyes rolled with excitement.

"This is MY party now!" he cried. *"But I don't WANT a birthday party! I want a WEDDING party! I'm ready to claim my bride! I'm ready to claim the one who will be my SLAVE for life!"*

I stared at him, my heart pounding. The sickening smell of the green gunk made my stomach churn.

"*I want my BRIDE!*" Slappy demanded at the top of his lungs. "*I want my bride — NOW!*"

"Okay!" I cried, my voice trembly and weak. "Okay. If we give you your bride, do you promise to go away with her? Do you promise you'll take her away and not hurt anyone here?"

The dummy's eyes flashed. He nodded his grinning, wooden head.

"*Yesssss,*" he hissed. "*I will take my bride away!*"

"Okay. Okay. Okay," I replied breathlessly, thinking hard. I turned to Harrison. "Give Slappy his bride," I instructed him.

Harrison gaped at me. "Huh?"

"His bride," I repeated, motioning with both hands. "Mary-Ellen. Give Slappy his bride."

"Oh." Harrison caught on. He raised Mary-Ellen in both hands. Then he crossed the room to Slappy. And handed the big doll to him.

Slappy stared at Mary-Ellen for a long moment.

Then, to my shock, he let out an angry growl — and heaved the doll across the basement.

"*Are you CRAZY?*" Slappy screamed. "*That ugly piece of junk! She can't be my bride!*"

Slappy reached out and grabbed me by the wrist.

"*Jillian, YOU are my bride!*" he cried.

"OW!" I cried out as the dummy's grip tightened round my wrist.

I tugged hard. Jerked my arm round. But I couldn't pull free.

Around the room, kids were screaming and crying. I saw two girls hugging each other against the wall, their legs trembling.

Eddie stood in the middle of the room hugging himself, his teeth chattering from fear.

I looked for Katie and Amanda. They were huddled by the stairs, covered in green goo.

Harrison stood in shock, his mouth hanging open. He took a step towards me, his trainers splashing in the green slime.

Grinning fiercely, Slappy tugged me closer. He pressed his wooden face against my ear.

"*You will be my slave,*" he whispered. "*You will be my slave for the rest of your life!*"

"No!" I screamed.

I tugged again. Tugged with all my strength to pull myself free.

But the evil dummy's grip tightened even more. I couldn't move.

I turned to Harrison. I opened my mouth to tell him to run up the stairs, to bring the parents from next door.

But before I could say a word, a voice rang out through the basement.

A female voice. An *angry* voice.

"*Let GO of that girl, Slappy!*" the voice cried. "*She isn't your bride! I AM!*"

I turned to see who was screaming.

Mary-Ellen!

Kids screamed and cried. Four girls huddled against the wall, hugging each other.

The big doll clomped across the floor, her frizzy hair flying behind her. She stomped right over two kids. Her hands were clenched into tight fists.

"You worthless stick of rotting wood!" she screamed at Slappy. She strode up to him and gave him a hard shove with both fists.

Startled, Slappy staggered back.

His hand slid off me. Rubbing my throbbing wrist, I backed away.

Mary-Ellen grabbed Slappy by the throat. *"I didn't bring you to life for HER!"* she exclaimed furiously. *"I am your bride!"*

"Huh?" I let out a gasp. I narrowed my eyes at the fierce doll. *"You* brought Slappy to life?" I choked out.

The doll nodded. She shook Slappy hard. *"You*

toothpick!" she snarled. *"I'll turn you into SAWDUST if you don't shape up!"*

As I gaped in shock, Katie and Amanda came running up to me.

"We wanted to tell you, Jillian," Katie sobbed. "But Mary-Ellen wouldn't let us. The first day Dad brought her home, she started talking to us. Ordering us around. She said if we told anyone, she'd hurt us. We didn't know what to do. We were so scared. We'd never had a doll who was really alive!"

"Mary-Ellen did *everything!"* Amanda cried. "She stuffed your lizard in Slappy's mouth. She broke the dishes and threw the spaghetti everywhere. She scribbled those messages in your room."

"She carried the dummy everywhere," Katie added. "Mary-Ellen *made* Amanda and me say it was the dummy who did everything. But Slappy wasn't alive — until the party! He was never alive! Mary-Ellen did *everything!"*

"She wanted to hurt you and get you in trouble," Amanda told me.

A doll and a dummy — both alive. Both evil. The room started to spin round me.

I turned to Mary-Ellen. "Why?" I choked out. "Why did you do all those things to me?"

The doll's red lips formed an angry sneer. "Because you said you hated me," she growled. "Because you never wanted the girls to take

116

me anywhere. You slapped me, Jillian, and threw me away, and shoved my head into the macaroni."

Mary-Ellen's eyes flared with fury. "Did you think I couldn't hear you?" she screamed. "I heard every word you said about me, Jillian. And so I used the dummy to fool you and take my revenge. I didn't bring him to life until tonight, just before the party. Our *wedding* party!"

Katie squeezed my hand. "Amanda and I wanted to tell you the truth," she sobbed. "But Mary-Ellen said she'd hurt us. She said we had to take care of her for ever."

"We hated her! But she made us take her everywhere," Amanda cried, taking my other hand. "She was so nasty to us!"

"*Enough talk!*" Mary-Ellen screeched. She spun Slappy round. "And now, Slappy and I will rule together. And you — Jillian — you will be our slave. I plan to make you suffer — for the rest of your life!"

She turned to Slappy. "Right, my darling? Am I right?"

"*No way!*" Slappy cried. "*No way!*"

He slid his arm back — and swung his fist into her jaw.

The wooden fist hit the doll's head with a loud *THUMP*.

Mary-Ellen uttered a shocked groan — and crumpled to the floor.

117

"I will rule!" Slappy declared, raising both hands high above his head in victory. "But not with an ugly *rag doll* like you!"

He stared down at Mary-Ellen, sprawled on her back on the floor. His evil grin grew wider. "Why don't you learn to say goo-goo?" he snarled. "Maybe someone will think you're *cute!*"

He pulled his big shoe back and gave her a hard kick in the side. "Someone take the baby dolly out and *burp* her!" he declared nastily.

He pulled back his foot and kicked the doll again.

Mary-Ellen didn't move.

Grinning in triumph, Slappy spun round and grabbed my wrist again. "Come with me!" he ordered.

"Let go of me! Let go!" I shrieked.

"Never!" he cried. "You are my bride now, Jillian. You will go wherever I tell you to go."

The wooden hand clamped harder around my wrist.

"Oww! You're *hurting* me!" I wailed. "Let go! Let go!"

He threw back his head and uttered a scornful laugh. "You're *hurting* me!" he cried in a high, babyish voice, mocking me.

Then, without warning, he swung his head against my forehead in a hard head-butt.

"Ohhhhh." I groaned as the pain shot through my head, down my entire body.

"*What's your PROBLEM, Jillian?*" the dummy demanded. "*That was just a LOVE TAP!*" He threw back his head in another high-pitched laugh.

My head spinning, I struggled to force down the panic that froze me, struggled to pull free.

But he squeezed my wrist until I screamed. "*You'll never get away, my bride!*" he screamed. "*Never!*"

Then, to my surprise, he released me. His heavy wooden hand shot up in the air. He cried out in shock.

I staggered back. Rubbed my aching wrist.

What had happened?

I lowered my gaze — and saw that Mary-Ellen had revived. She had grabbed Slappy's legs. Pulled him away from me. And jerked him down to the floor.

The kids screamed and cried. Katie and

Amanda huddled together against the wall. I stumbled back to Harrison as the doll and the dummy began to fight.

They wrestled over the floor, rolling over and over through the disgusting green goo. Punching at each other, scratching, biting.

Up on their feet, their arms tightening around each other, they wrestled, shoved each other against the walls, stumbled over terrified kids, knocked over the two wooden stools, toppled the birthday cake to the floor.

Grunting and moaning, they wrestled, tearing at each other, slapping, pulling each other over the sticky green goo.

Into Dad's workshop.

I stumbled after them. They bounced off the work table. Stumbled over the coffee table Dad had been working on for so long. Rolled on top of it, spreading green gunk over the polished wood.

And then . . . then . . . it all happened so fast.

I saw Slappy's hand shoot out. Saw him flick on the buzz-saw.

The roar of the big saw made me cover my ears with my hands.

And as I stared in shock, my hands to my head, I saw Slappy shove Mary-Ellen . . . shove her . . . shove her into the whirring buzz-saw blade.

The saw whined — a deafening, shrill whine — as it cut the big doll in half.

The blade sawed through her easily. Her bottom half — her legs, her skirt — dropped to the floor beside the big saw.

Slappy threw back his head. And laughed. Laughed in triumph. His laughter rose above the roar of the saw.

And then his laugh cut short. His grin faded. The dummy's eyes bulged in horror.

Mary-Ellen's top half held on to Slappy.

Her hands gripped him . . . gripped him tightly. And *pulled him through the whirring saw blade*!

The blade sliced Slappy across the waist. Sliced him in half.

Both halves fell to the floor.

I stared down at the doll and the dummy. Both sliced in half.

Both lifeless now. Lifeless once again.

Struggling to catch my breath, to slow my pounding heart, I clicked off the saw. The blade whirred silently, slowing to a stop.

I let out a long sigh of relief. Stared down at the lifeless doll, the lifeless dummy. Lying so still now.

Walking on trembling legs, I stared down at Slappy. Bent over his top half. Bent down to make sure he had no life left in him.

And his hand shot up — and grabbed my leg.

28

"Ohhhhh!" I uttered a cry of horror. I fell back.

Slappy's hand crumpled. Clunked lifelessly to the floor.

He didn't move again.

I took a deep breath and held it. I shut my eyes and counted to ten, struggling to calm myself.

A commotion behind me made me open my eyes and spin round. I saw Harrison running down the stairs. Several parents followed him. I realized he had run next door to get them.

Kids were screaming and crying. I hugged Katie and Amanda.

Mum and Dad stopped halfway down the stairs. "Jillian — what's all the noise?" Mum called. "What is this disgusting mess?"

"Well," I replied, "it's a bit of a long story. . ."

"Harrison — what are you doing with that?" I asked.

"Just reading it," he replied.

It was nearly ten o'clock that night. I was finally starting to feel better. My heartbeat had returned to normal. My legs had stopped trembling.

We had spent the rest of the day apologizing to Mrs Simkin and the other parents. Then we all pitched in to clean up the basement.

Mum and Dad were still demanding a full explanation. I wasn't sure how I could ever explain.

Now, Harrison and I were on the sofa in the study. Katie and Amanda were sprawled on the floor, watching TV.

Harrison was leaning over the ventriloquist's diary, reading it slowly, carefully, with great interest.

"I can't believe you stole that old diary," I said.

He raised a finger to his lips. "Sshhh. This is very interesting."

I groaned. "Why are you still reading that thing? It's all over. We don't have anything more to worry about."

"I'm not so sure," Harrison replied softly.

"Huh? What do you mean?" I demanded.

"Listen to what the diary says," Harrison replied. "It says that even if the dummy is destroyed, the evil may not die."

"Huh?" I cried. "It says *what*?"

Harrison held the little book closer to read it. "It says the dummy's body may be destroyed — but the evil spirit may not be killed. It will just move on to another body."

I shook my head. "Well, that's ridiculous," I said. "Slappy is dead. Dead, dead, dead."

Harrison shrugged. "The diary says the evil can be passed to someone who was close to the dummy."

I turned to Katie and Amanda. "That's ridiculous — isn't it, girls?"

They looked up from the TV and grinned at Harrison and me.

I narrowed my eyes and studied them. Why do they have such strange grins on their faces? I wondered.

I stared at them for a long while.

"Harrison," I whispered. "Guess what? I'm finally going to get my revenge."

I tilted back my head, opened my mouth wide, turned to my sisters — and spewed thick green gunk all over them.